THE MAGNOLIA CAFE

KAY CORRELL

ROSE QUARTZ PRESS

Published by Rose Quartz Press

r091217

ISBN: 978-1-944761-04-2

KAY'S BOOKS

Find more information on all my books at *kaycorrell.com*

COMFORT CROSSING ~ THE SERIES
The Shop on Main - Book One
The Memory Box - Book Two
The Christmas Cottage - A Holiday Novella (Book 2.5)
The Letter - Book Three
The Christmas Scarf - A Holiday Novella (Book 3.5)
The Magnolia Cafe - Book Four
The Unexpected Wedding - Book Five

The Wedding in the Grove - (a crossover short story between series - with Josephine and Paul from The Letter.)

LIGHTHOUSE POINT ~ THE SERIES
Wish Upon a Shell - Book One
Wedding on the Beach - Book Two

Love at the Lighthouse - Book Three

INDIGO BAY ~ A multi-author sweet romance series
Sweet Sunrise - Book Three

Sign up for my newsletter at my website *kaycorrell.com* to make sure you don't miss any new releases or sales.

CHAPTER 1

Keely Granger clenched her teeth and pasted on what she hoped was a semi-good attempt at a smile. Keely spun around, menus in hand, at the sound of yet more customers entering the cafe.

"Hi, there's about a twenty minute wait. Is that okay?" They were doing a brisk business tonight. Which was good and bad. The new waitress had called in sick for the second time in a week and a half. Keely was going to do a remarkable job of chewing out the new waitress—if she ever showed up for work again. Becky Lee, their dependable long-time waitress, was doing the work of two servers. That left Keely doing triple duty as hostess, manager, and backup server tonight.

"We'll catch you another time then, Keely."

Keely watched as a family of four headed down Main Street in search of another place to eat where they didn't have to wait for a table, or at the very least had an area where they could wait for their table without sitting outside on the wooden benches that made up Magnolia Cafe's "waiting area."

Keely set the menus back down on the counter. She hurried off to grab a tray of water glasses, pausing at the table near the door to pick up dirty dishes. They needed a bus person, too, at least on the weekend nights. Of course if the new waitress would show up, that would help. She tilted her head from side to side, trying to release some of the tension of the day.

"I'll get that." Becky Lee swooped in and picked up the tray of water glasses. "Headed back there to take their order anyway." The waitress smiled at her as if she knew that Keely was feeling overwhelmed tonight.

The evening wore on. And on. A smile for a customer here, handling a complaint there. It was always the same thing night after night. Different people each night, but the same routine.

Hours later Keely looked up when she caught a glance of a tall man standing in the doorway. Hunt Robichaux. She hadn't seen him in years. Last she'd heard he was off traveling the world, the lucky duck.

She secretly kept track of him, mainly because she'd always wished things could have been different, that she could have been his sidekick off writing travel articles while he shot his photography. They had such plans when they were growing up. A dynamic duo of travel writer and travel photographer. She'd so wanted to live the life he'd made for himself.

"Hey, Hunt. Long time no see." She walked over and gave him a quick hug.

"It has been a while. Looks like you're keeping busy here." Hunt nodded towards the remaining tables of customers. "I drove by earlier and there were people waiting outside on the benches."

And that had obviously chased him away. Keely told herself for the millionth time she had to convince her mother that adding a covered patio area behind the restaurant was a smart move. People would be much more willing to have a drink out on the patio, and less likely to leave when the wait time grew longer on the weekends. It was a brilliant idea of hers, even if her mom wouldn't admit it. Her mom rarely worked at the restaurant any more, but vetoed just about any change Keely wanted to make.

"We were busy tonight." *We need to do something to be busier more often, you know, if we had anywhere for people to wait for a table.* But, of course, she couldn't admit that to Hunt. He'd made something out of his life. She'd seen his photography over the years. First in regional magazines and papers, then in national magazines. Someone was always bringing in a copy to show her. In a small town like Comfort Crossing, Mississippi everyone knew she and Hunt had been good friends from grade school through high school.

"You want a table by the window?"

"Actually, I was wondering if you have some of that chicken noodle soup you always used to have? My sister is sick. I thought that might help. I don't know what else to do for her. I'd be fine with canned soup, but she'd never go for that."

"We sure do. Come on back to the kitchen, I'll get it

for you. We just put a big pot of it in the fridge. You'll just have to heat it for her."

"Thanks."

Hunt followed her back into the kitchen. "Not much has changed here, huh?"

"Not much." That was an understatement. Nothing ever changed in this town. Though Hunt sure had changed. He looked so different than he had growing up. Older—in a worldly way. He'd lost the boyish look of his teens and replaced it with a self-confident look of a thirty-something who had seen things and done things and moved on from small town life.

He'd aged well. His thick brown hair was a touch longer than he used to wear it. He was in great shape, he looked like he was one of those guys who could do a hundred pushups without breaking a sweat. She was lucky to find enough time to consider walking back and forth to the cafe as exercise.

She reached for the to-go containers for the soup. "What brings you back to town?"

"I came back to help my sister out for a bit. She's having a hard time after losing Kevin."

"I miss him, too. It was all so terrible, and it happened so fast. I can't imagine losing your husband like that, so young."

"Natalie's still reeling. I couldn't make it back for Kevin's funeral, I was halfway around the world. It took them a week just to track me down. I feel terrible about that. I wound up my assignment and came back as fast as I could, but I had to leave right away again.

Commitments. But I got that all sorted out and I'm back for a while."

Keely sighed. Life was sometimes so unfair. Her sister, Katherine, knew that. Natalie knew that. Yet, they both went on with their lives as best they could. And just like that, the pity party Keely had been having tonight whisked away into the night.

Kevin had been a great guy. Not only when they were all friends in high school, but later. He'd come by and fixed things for her at the cafe before, always offering to help with something. Never taking more than a free meal for payment.

"How are the kids?"

"Well, they miss their dad."

"I bet. It's really all so sad."

Hunt and Kevin had been inseparable when they were kids. It must be hitting him hard now too, but nothing showed in his eyes. He'd always been able to keep his emotions under wraps. She'd always admired that about him.

Hunt raked his hand through his hair. "Now Natalie is sick, and I'm trying to figure out how to take care of the kids and her. Not my strongest suit."

Keely handed him the soup. "Well, try this. Hope it helps."

He stood up and smiled. Same rakish grin from his youth, that much hadn't changed. "So how is Katherine doing?"

Keely never really knew how to answer that question when people asked her about her sister. "As well as can be expected. She finally graduated college this year. She's really happy about that."

"Good for her. I should drop by and see her."

"She'd like that."

"So, how much do I owe you?"

"Nothing. It's on me. A welcome home present."

"Thanks, I appreciate it."

"Come by again soon and we'll catch up."

"Will do."

Keely walked him to the front door. He nodded as he slipped back out into the night. The lights from the street lamps on Main Street illuminated the parking spaces. She watched him climb into a pickup truck and pull away. Traveling the world taking pictures. Now that would be the life. She wondered how long he planned on staying here in town. Not long she'd bet. Why would anyone stay here who had a better offer anywhere else in the world?

Keely turned back to the tables filled with the last of their customers. She paused and looked at the patrons all laughing and talking. Enjoying each other. Having lives. She sighed again, hadn't she just told herself enough of the pity party?

An hour later, Keely pushed the door closed behind the last customer and told Becky Lee to go on home. Exhaustion washed over her. She wanted to total the days' receipts, lock the place up, and head for home. Her mother was probably waiting there, playing cards with Katherine. Her mom no longer stayed at the cafe past about eight o'clock in the evenings. She always said

Katherine couldn't be left alone for very long. Then she'd shoot a meaningful glance Keely's direction.

That left Keely to lock up. Every night. At least they were closed on Monday nights. One night a week to herself. Which she usually spent collapsed in a heap of exhaustion, or even more likely, buried in bookwork that she hadn't completed. Bills, taxes, more bills, invoices, ordering food, more bills. It went on and on. Year after year.

She flipped the sign in the front window from open to closed. She figured she'd probably done that over four thousand times in the fifteen years she'd run the restaurant for her family. Well, and another four thousand plus times opening the cafe back up the next day.

This was not how she'd planned her life. It was how life had grabbed her and held her, imprisoned her in a grasp too tight to break.

Hunt drove the short distance to his sister's house and pulled into the gravel driveway. The house was set back from the street, framed by two large live oak trees that shaded the deep Acadian porch. The house stood peaceful and quiet, a marked contrast to the raucous hotel he'd stayed in on his last assignment. He wasn't exactly envious of her life. It was such a hard time for her now, full of the responsibility of raising her sons on her own.

It kicked him in the gut that Kevin was gone. They'd been friends since grade school. He missed the guy. He could only imagine how much Natalie missed Kevin.

Hunt had been thrilled when Natalie and Kevin had hooked up after high school and gotten married less than a year later. It had given Hunt peace of mind to know Kevin would be looking after his sister while he, himself, was off roaming around the world, taking his photos. Besides, Hunt had proven long ago he was a horrible caretaker, unable to keep people safe and well. Kevin had done a great job with the responsibility of a family. Well, until he'd died and left Natalie to deal with everything.

Hunt strode up the front steps to the front door. Jamie, Jackson, and Jesse came rushing at him. "Hey, you said you'd be gone thirty minutes. It's been an hour." Jamie had learned to tell time, obviously.

"Sorry, kiddo. I had to stop and fill up the truck and had a few errands to run."

He stopped in the kitchen, poured the soup into a bowl, and popped it into the microwave. Now, heating things up in the microwave, that he knew how to do.

He opened and closed cabinet doors until he found a tray. He loaded the tray with the bowl of soup, a few crackers, and a glass of water. He carried it out to the family room with Jamie in his wake.

"You didn't have to do all this, Hunt. I'll be fine." Natalie huddled under a quilt on the couch. He looked around the brightly lit room. A room that begged a person to come in, sit down, relax. He was sure his sister could turn any space into a home. The boys' things were spilled around the room. An overstuffed chair set diagonally across the corner with a bright reading light beside it. Next to the chair was his sister's ever present knitting bag. She was always working on something. He'd a stack of sweaters to prove it.

Over the couch hung a water color painting of an Adirondack chair at the edge of the ocean. A straw hat with a bright pink ribbon was lying in the sand beside the chair. His sister loved the ocean. She had a set of three framed photographs he'd taken of beaches around the world. Her touch was everywhere, from the vase of flowers on the end table, to the braided rag rug on the floor. How she'd gotten the make-a-house-a-home gene, he'd never understand.

Hunt crossed the room. "Well, it's not like I know how to make homemade soup for you. Hope you can keep this down. You haven't eaten in days." He turned to the boys. "Aren't you boys supposed to be getting ready for bed?"

"It's too early for me to go to bed, Uncle Hunt." Jackson gave him a look of disdain.

Jackson had not been impressed with his uncle's parenting abilities. Well, Hunt wasn't trying to parent. He'd settle for uncle-ing. Now what was he supposed to do? Was Jackson testing him yet again?

"Okay then. How about this? Jamie and Jesse, you go get ready for bed. Jackson, you go get ready, but you can come back downstairs and watch TV for a bit."

"I'm not going to bed, if Jackson's not." Jesse stood

with his hand on his hip looking so much like Kevin that it sucked the air right out of Hunt's lungs. He struggled to regain his composure.

"That's it," Natalie interrupted from the couch. "Everyone upstairs and in their jammies. Uncle Hunt will be up to tuck you in. Jackson, you can read for half an hour, or go on to bed now. Your choice."

"Mom…"

"Don't Mom me."

The two older boys headed up the stairs. His sister made it seem so easy.

Jamie tromped over and hugged Natalie. "'Night, Mom. Hope you feel good soon."

"'Night, sweetie. Sleep tight."

The boys all clomped up the stairs and Hunt could hear them scuffling around as they got ready for bed. "I'm not sure how you do it, Nat."

"Do what?"

"Handle those three boys, the house…"

"I don't really have a choice." She sighed. "It's been hard. I miss Kevin. And I've got to get a job. The bills are piling up."

"I'll help out with the bills and I'll stay as long as you need me."

"I'm not going to be your burden."

"You're not a burden. I want to help. Besides, I miss the boys. And you."

"The boys are beasts." Natalie grinned and took a sip of the soup.

"That they are."

He went upstairs and tucked the boys in. Jamie gave

him specific instructions on what all was involved in the process. Tuck in the covers, read him one short book, turn out the light, leave the door halfway open and the hall light on. Who knew it was such a complicated business to put a kid to bed?

By the time he got to Jesse's room, the boy was already sound asleep. He looked so peaceful. It was hard to believe he could be such a ball of energy all day long, creating havoc in his wake, and then crash with an illusion of an angel on his face. Hunt tucked the covers around the boy and switched off the bedside lamp.

He poked his head into Jackson's room and said good night then went downstairs to clean up the mess that always seemed to follow in the wake of the boys.

He picked up empty glasses and one half full one, a plate from the coffee table, a gum wrapper off the floor. The boys had been playing a video game in the front room, and he switched off the game and the TV. A simple quiet settled over the house. Natalie had drifted back to sleep. He guessed that was a good thing, because the sooner she recovered, the sooner she could take care of the boys before he managed to make some big mistake with them.

He'd come here to help her out, but to be honest, his knowledge of raising kids was limited. More than limited. Oh, he could mow the yard, take care of the truck, make some needed repairs around the house, but as far as helping with the boys, he was clueless. He was trying his best, but he always felt they were getting the better of him and he was pretty sure they knew it.

～

Keely walked home from the cafe. It was only a short three block walk to their two story home on Juniper Street. She liked walking home at night and unwinding from the stress of the day. Comfort Crossing was a safe town, well as safe as a town could be these days. She walked down Main Street and cut across Fourth Street to Juniper. The moonlight filtered through the large old trees lining the street. A slight breeze had picked up, chilling the air. She quickened her pace, mentally reminding herself it was still sweater weather this time of year and to bring one tomorrow when she left for work.

She climbed up the porch steps and push through the front door. "Hey, Mother. I'm home."

Really, should a woman of her age be saying that every night?

"We're in here, Keely."

Keely walked into the family room where her sister and mom sat half-watching the end of the evening news. Her mother had the inevitable crossword puzzle held in her lap, a mechanical pencil clipped to the precisely folded newspaper. "What's an eight letter word for trapped?"

My life? No, wait that was two words, and not enough letters. Kelly dropped her purse by the end of the couch.

"Starts with the letter C."

"Cornered." She was good at this synonym for her life thing.

"Good business tonight?" Katherine looked up from

the book she was reading, her blonde hair spilling across her shoulders in the lamplight.

"Pretty brisk." Keely looked over at her sister and for a moment could almost picture her as she was when they were teenagers. Vibrant. Alive. The captain of the cheerleading squad, instead of shackled to the chrome and black wheelchair that was her constant companion now.

"You need any help before I head off to bed?" Keely just wanted to crash, but had to at least offer to help Katherine.

"No, I'm fine. I think I'll stay up a bit and catch a movie. I'm not very tired tonight."

"Well, call upstairs if you need me."

Keely walked past her sister's bedroom, the room that used to be her father's den. They'd converted it to a bedroom with a wheelchair accessible bathroom after Katherine's accident. Terms like wheelchair accessible had become part of their daily vocabulary after the accident. That along with the long ramp up the side of the front porch were constant reminders of how their lives had all changed that one night fifteen years ago.

All her plans had gone up in smoke. Well, her sister's plans too, if she was being honest. Keely had planned to go away to college. She'd gotten a scholarship to the University of Missouri to study journalism. Katherine was going to finish up high school and then step in and learn to run the restaurant. Instead, Katherine had had multiple surgeries and physical therapy, and Keely had stayed home to help her parents with the cafe. The family's finances had been stretched thin. Then her father had died of a heart attack just one year later. The entire responsibility of the restaurant—and the family's entire income—fell directly on Keely's shoulders. Which is where it belonged. Because the whole mess that was their lives was all her fault.

CHAPTER 2

Keely smacked the button on the top of her alarm. She needed to get moving early today. She scrunched the pillow up behind her head and sat up in bed, leaning against the headboard. A few moments to pull herself together, and she'd be okay. The bird outside her window sang a cheerful good morning, as usual. Keely had put up bird feeders in the backyard. She loved to sit in the window seat in her room and stare out at the birds flitting around the yard, soaring off to unknown places. Their bubbly morning melody raised her spirits.

A rosy glow of the morning light filtered into her room. The same view she'd woken up to her entire life. The same quilt on the same twin bed, the same lace curtains hung over the windows. Her desk that used to hold homework, now spilled over with bookwork from the restaurant. Her old stereo had been replaced with a small MP3 player and speakers, mostly because she needed the room on top of her dresser to stack up yet more files and printouts from work.

The bedroom walls were a faded yellow now. She kept thinking she'd change that, but really, when did she have the time for something as superfluous as painting her room? She only used the room for crashing out in exhaustion anyway.

She needed an attitude adjustment, she knew that. Another day feeling sorry for herself wasn't going to change anything. It just wasted her time and made her annoyed at herself.

Listen to the birds. They are exuberantly greeting the day. Learn from them.

She leaned over to the bedside table and slipped her journal out of the drawer. The journal was a brightly colored flowered notebook. She was writing in it with her favorite fountain pen and bright pink ink. She scoured the stores and searched online for just the right notebooks for her journals. Fountain pens and expensive journals were the two extravagances she allowed herself. To her they were much more exciting than new shoes or designer purses. She obsessively coordinated the ink color with the cover of each journal. She had her favorite fountain pens, always with a fine nib, and too many bottles of ink to count. An entire box of journals were hidden in the back of her closet dated back to the year she turned thirteen. Sometimes she thought they were the only reason she was still sane. If anyone would call her sane.

Keely opened the notebook and started writing. She carefully wrote the date, the day of the week, and the weather. Just as always. Her words flowed neatly across the lined pages. Then she wrote down the first thing that popped into her mind. *I saw Hunt Robichaux again. He's looking good.*

Hunt stretched and looked out the window at the early morning daybreak. A warm pink color filtered upward from the horizon. He sat up and looked around the converted porch he was using for a room. Well, he'd stayed in much worse places in his travels. He'd never really had a place to call home, not even growing up. They'd moved constantly around town. Each time to a smaller and smaller house, finally to a beat up two room apartment where he slept on the couch and lived out of two cardboard boxes tucked into the corner. Natalie had had a closet sized room, and his parents a room not much bigger.

Until everything had fallen apart, that is. That crappy two bedroom walkup had looked like easy street compared to life after that.

He couldn't really afford to stay here too long, though. All he knew how to do was shoot photos, and he was pretty darn good at it. He loved photography. Seeing just the right light. Capturing emotions on film, and now digitally.

Even though Natalie needed help, he wasn't sure he could trade something he was talented at and proud of, for some nine-to-five job here in town. Besides, what the heck would he do? He wasn't even sure he was that much help to Natalie, she certainly couldn't rely on his parenting skills.

He knew his sister had been looking for a job, too. Things were tight around here without Kevin's income. Hunt had some savings he'd be glad to share with his sister, but she was probably too proud to accept his help. She'd always been one to make her way on her own. Heck, so had he. Cut from the same cloth. It's not like they really had anyone to depend on growing up. Their mom had been too sick, and their dad… well, he wasn't much interested in raising kids, or supporting his family, for that matter. Hunt tried to hold it all together for Natalie and his mom, but he'd failed at that.

Spectacularly.

He rolled over on his side and stared out across the backyard. Kevin had cleared an area around the house and planted pecan trees down the slope of the hill out back. He'd fenced an area near the house and built the boys a tree house. All the things a dad should do for his kids, not that Hunt's dad had done any of that.

It wasn't fair Kevin was gone now, a really great dad, and the boys would grow up with barely a distant memory of him. Especially Jamie, at six years old he wasn't going to have many memories to hold onto.

He swung his legs over the edge of the bed, grabbed his jeans, and tugged them on. It still surprised him he was back in Comfort Crossing, something he vowed would never happen.

A fleeting picture of Keely flashed through his mind, how she'd looked last night. Tired, but good. He'd always thought she'd go off and travel the world. She must have decided to stay here in Comfort Crossing after Katherine's accident. He wondered if she ever regretted that decision.

Keely looked about the same as she had in high school. Long brown hair, though she'd had it pulled back in some kind of efficient braid type thing. She'd walked through the restaurant, so confident, just like she owned the place. He laughed to himself. Well, he guessed she did own the place, at least partially.

She was different in some ways, too. Not the carefree girl who ran with the same crowd of friends he did growing up. Hunt had tried so hard to fit in with that crowd, pretend he was an untroubled, happy-go-lucky kid like they all were, trying to make life easier on Natalie so she'd at least a chance of a normal life. He shook his head. Failures. This town just made him think of all of his failures. He couldn't leave town fast enough. Though, Natalie could use his help getting settled into her new life, so he'd promised himself he'd at least stay a bit. A short bit. Before Natalie started to rely on him and he'd a chance to screw that up.

His thoughts bounced back to Keely. He tried to remember if she'd dated anyone in high school. She must have, but he couldn't remember anyone special.

She'd looked tired last night, like the weight of the world was on her shoulders. It must be a lot of responsibility to manage Magnolia Cafe and keep everything running smoothly. He bet it was the only income that Keely, Katherine, and their mom had.

Just then Jamie came bursting into the sunroom.

"Hey, Uncle Hunt. I'm starving. What are you making for breakfast?"

He gathered Jamie up and tossed him over his shoulder. "Let's go see, kiddo."

Keely slipped the key into the lock on the front door and pushed into the Magnolia Cafe promptly at six o'clock. They opened at six thirty, but she had a lot to get done today. She was behind on the bill paying, mainly because she was juggling funds to make ends meet. She needed to do the paychecks for the week, too. She needed a few minutes to get organized before their early morning regulars came into the cafe. Frank, Bob, and Eddie came in and sat at the same table in the corner before heading off to their various jobs. Sue Lake dropped in to grab coffee and a quick bite to eat most mornings before heading over to the high school where she taught history. Widow Schneider came by later in the mornings for her hot tea, toast, and company. Melanie, the cook, usually invited Miz Schneider back to chat in the kitchen while she worked on the lunch items.

She inhaled the scent of cinnamon filling the cafe, announcing their famous cinnamon rolls were already baking. She was darn lucky to have found Melanie, an excellent cook and an early riser to boot. Melanie slipped in early and started baking at five each morning, Tuesday through Saturday. Melanie said her Sundays were for going to church. So on Sundays Keely had a string of part-time cooks that came and went. Mostly went. She'd been known to put on an apron and be the cook herself on Sunday. Thankfully, Melanie got extra pies and rolls made on Saturday afternoons that they used for their Sunday customers.

"Hey, Melanie. Smells good."

"You want one? There's a batch already out of the oven." Melanie waved a spatula in the general direction of the cinnamon rolls. "And the coffee's made."

"Thanks." Keely grabbed a cinnamon roll. Icing rolled down the sides like icicles hanging from a roof. Not that she'd seen that in person, because it sure didn't get cold enough in Comfort Crossing, Mississippi to have icicles. After pouring a steaming cup of coffee— black, of course, nothing frou-frou in her coffee—she headed for her office.

The morning sped by and the errant waitress who didn't show up last night arrived late with excuses for her no show and why she was late this morning. Keely knew she had to deal with her. Fire her. Find someone new. They just couldn't keep working shorthanded. Thank goodness for reliable, even keel, Becky Lee. She'd been with them for years, always dependable, and the customers loved her.

The new waitress wasn't watching where she was going—too busy eyeing the Johnson boy—and bumped into Keely. The tray the girl was carrying crashed to floor along with dirty dishes and glasses. The girl looked at Keely expectantly, like she thought her boss would clean up the mess.

Keely nodded towards the kitchen. "There's a broom by the back door."

The waitress stalked off to find it with one last look at the Johnson boy.

Keely stepped over the mess and headed over to the register. She looked up and saw Hunt and Natalie walk through the front door, with Natalie's three boys in tow. "Hi, table for five?"

"Hey, Keely. The boys are starving and they're tired of my breakfasts." Hunt ruffled the hair on his youngest nephew's head.

"All Uncle Hunt makes for breakfast is cereal," the oldest boy said. What was his name? Jackson? Jeremy? Jason? She knew it was a J name. She never could keep them straight.

"And we're out of cereal," the youngest boy chimed in. Jamie. She could remember his name. He looked like a Jamie. Quick impish grin and a smattering of freckles across his nose.

"I haven't had time to go to the market. I'm just starting to feel better. I'll shop after we get these boys fed and dropped off at school."

"I told you I could have shopped for you, Nat," Hunt insisted.

"Yes, like last time. You came home with so much junk food and forgot the milk. I think I'll stick to doing the shopping."

"We rock, paper, scissored, and I won." The other J-named boy chimed in. "So I got to pick where we get to eat. I picked here 'cause I love Miss Melanie's cinnamon rolls."

"Well, come on in and we'll get you boys a big breakfast then."

The always-have-an-excuse waitress walked up and interrupted. "Keely, I have to go. Something came up."

"I need you here. You're the only waitress on the schedule with me." *And you have a mess to clean up.*

"Well, I quit then."

Keely sighed. The girl hadn't lasted a week. "Okay, come to my office and sign a form that says you're quitting." Keely had learned a lot in the years running the business. Like if an employee said they quit, have them sign a resignation, so they didn't come back and say she fired them.

Just then another large group of customers came through the door. Natalie jumped up from the table. "Here, let me get them. I'll seat them over at that big round table in the corner, okay?"

"That'd be great, thanks." Keely smiled at Natalie in relief.

By the time Keely got back out from her office, she saw Natalie with a gray plastic bin balanced on her hip, clearing the broken dishes off the floor.

"You don't have to do that."

"I don't mind. You look like you can use the help."

"I can. Want a job?" Keely asked only half-joking.

"I do need a job. And I'd love one if I can figure out what to do with the boys."

"Really?"

"I have experience. I waitressed in high school. Let me help you this morning and see how it goes. I'm sure Hunt will take the boys to school."

They walked over to where Hunt and the boys were waiting for her at the front door. Natalie caught Jesse just before he had a chance to shoot the wrapper off a straw. "I don't think so Jesse. You boys go on outside."

The three boys pushed out into the sunshine and leapt up on the benches outside the door. "Hunt, could you take the boys to school? I'm going to stay and help out Keely."

"Really?"

"Really. I need a job. She's going to give me a try."

"That's great. I'll help out with the boys." A look of something crossed Hunt's face. Not exactly reluctance, not exactly enthusiasm either. Maybe a hint of panic?

"Well, I'll need to find someone to take care of them if I take this job. It's not your responsibility to watch them. Besides, you'll be leaving soon."

Hunt looked a bit relieved. "We'll talk about it after you get home."

"Thanks, Hunt. You're a sweetie."

"Yes, I really appreciate this, Hunt. Your sister is a lifesaver. That waitress kept leaving me shorthanded. You know, for the one week she worked for me. And I use the word *worked* loosely."

"Okay then, I'll see you later at home, Nat."

Keely and Natalie watched for a moment while Hunt shoved through the door and tried to corral the boys into the truck. Natalie pushed the door open. "Boys, in the truck. Now."

The three boys hopped right into the vehicle and Hunt shook his head.

CHAPTER 3

B ecky Lee loved working with Natalie. The woman could juggle six things at once and not blink an eye. It had been a long time since they'd had a good, reliable waitress at the cafe. She'd begun to feel guilty of any days she wasn't working, because that left Keely with inexperienced waitresses more interested in flirting with the men than waiting the tables. She couldn't remember the last time Keely had taken a day off, either.

She and Natalie had worked the lunch shift with no trouble, keeping up with the constant stream of customers.

"Natalie, if Keely hasn't said so, I will. You are a lifesaver."

"I hope this works out. I have to figure out childcare for the boys after school, though. I'll have to sort that all out. But I'm grateful for the job. It's time I got out of the house, too. I've just been existing since Kevin…"

"We'll sure keep you busy. I can promise you that."

Becky Lee sat down at the counter with a tray of silverware and a stack of napkins and started rolling silverware in the napkins for the dinner rush.

"Here, let me help." Natalie started to sit down.

"No, hon. You've worked a good long shift for your first day. I'm sure you're ready to go home and put your feet up."

"I admit that. I need to find some more comfortable shoes to wear. I'll go talk to Keely and see when she wants me to come back tomorrow."

"Okay, I'll see you then." Becky Lee efficiently rolled the napkin rolls. She'd been doing it for years. She could probably do it in her sleep. She finished up the post lunch chores and glanced around the cafe. Two tables were still filled with people sipping coffee. Tonight Keely had two part-time waitresses working with her. At least Tuesday nights were usually slow. Becky Lee would offer to stay, but she'd made plans with her best friends, Jenny and Izzy. They were going to work on plans for Jenny's upcoming wedding to Clay.

Becky Lee said goodbye to Keely and hurried out the door to walk home. She was having her friends over for dinner tonight. She had most of the food already made and had baked an almond cake she wanted Jenny to try in case she'd like that for her wedding cake. The warmth of the afternoon sun surrounded her. She loved this time of year before the hot, humid heat of the summer made everything unbearably muggy.

She walked up the steps to her cottage and pushed inside. She hooked her purse on the coat tree by the door, opening windows as she headed to the kitchen.

She loved her little kitchen with its gas stove, the red formica-topped table that Izzy had found for her, and a big window overlooking her backyard herb garden.

She opened the fridge and grabbed the pitcher of sweet tea. She poured it into one of her much loved but mismatched glasses and took a sip. She had just enough time to change clothes and finish up getting things ready for her friends.

Jenny and Isabella—Bella to most of the town, and Izzy to Jenny and Becky Lee—climbed the steps to Becky Lee's cute little cottage. With a quick rap on the door, they both went inside.

"Back here," Becky Lee called from the kitchen. "Be out in a minute."

Jenny and Izzy wandered back to the kitchen. "Smells delicious." Jenny peered over her friend's shoulder trying to see what Becky Lee had made. Becky Lee was the cook of the three friends. She cooked, she baked, and she came up with the most delicious concoctions.

"I hope you don't mind eating here in the kitchen. Or we could eat out on the patio, though the temperature has dropped since this afternoon. I heard we're going to have a run of chilly days again."

"Eating in the kitchen is fine." Izzy dropped a three-ring binder on the counter. "I've got lots of ideas for Jenny's wedding. Pulled some things together to show you."

Becky Lee nodded toward the refrigerator. "Jenny, you want to pour us some wine? I have it chilling in the fridge."

Jenny walked over to the cabinets and pulled out three wine glasses, then opened the refrigerator and saw a bottle of pinot blanc that Becky Lee had chilled. She pulled it out and poured each of them a glass.

"Let's go sit in the front room while dinner finishes. We'll go over the plans and see what we still need to do." Becky Lee took a glass of the wine and led the way to the front room. Jenny took a sip of wine and followed her friend.

Jenny sat on the couch, glad to be off her feet. It had been a long day at school. Her students were getting antsy as spring break grew near. She didn't blame them. She was ready for break to start herself. Especially with her wedding coming up, there was so much to do.

Izzy opened the binder with her ever growing checklist. "Okay. Becky Lee has the menu all planned with Sylvia. We'll have the reception at Sylvia's Place in her new upstairs room she's opened for events and receptions. Becky Lee, any final decision on the cake?"

"I've made one more cake for you to try tonight, then Jenny will have to decide."

Jenny didn't know how she would have ever pulled off this wedding without all the help from her friends. Izzy was the ultimate planner and had organized so much. She'd even found a vintage wedding dress and altered it for Jenny to wear.

"I'll be glad for spring break so I can just concentrate on the wedding. Danielle and Abigail want me to take them shopping for dresses for the wedding. Kind of an almost-stepmother-daughter thing. They said Clay wasn't a good dress shopper, and I couldn't agree more. The man hates to shop, so it will be a fun outing for the girls. I think I'll take them into New Orleans. Nathan needs new dress pants and a dress shirt, too. I swear that boy of mine outgrows clothes every week. I thought they slowed down their growth spurts in high school." Jenny took another sip of the wine, her mind whirling with all the things she needed to do.

"Write them down, Jenny." Izzy laughed and handed her friend a sheet of paper and a pen.

"I wish I were as organized as you. I can't seem to get everything done that needs to be done."

"When are you going to move?" Becky Lee glanced at her watch.

"We're going to move almost everything next month, but Nathan and I will wait to move until after the wedding. A bit old fashioned, but I just wouldn't feel right moving in with the kids and everything. Not before we make it official."

"Ah, your old-fashioned ways are part of your charm." Izzy grinned at her and looked down at her binder. "Okay, moving on. We'll have the wedding in the backyard of my carriage house. I've got some rental chairs ordered and I'll do up a nice arbor for you. Gil is going to build it for me. It pays to have a handy brother. Hopefully the weather will cooperate, but just in case, I'm going to find a backup plan."

"You think of everything." Jenny was filled with

gratitude for all the help, for their years and years of friendship.

"I found a place to order the flowers you wanted. Simple white hydrangeas. They will look wonderful." Izzy looked at her list again. "Becky Lee and I still need to get our dresses. We just need to finalize the color and we'll get different style dresses, but the same color."

"You two will make great tandem maids of honor."

"Way to go, not having to pick between us." Becky Lee grinned.

"As if I ever could. You two are the best."

"We are." Izzy nodded gravely then the corners of her mouth teased into a grin. "Good thing you have us. Oh, and Owen is going to work with Sylvia to pick the wines for the reception, if that's okay. I'm good at planning, but I just don't know wines and how much we need to order."

"How is Owen? Back in town again?"

"I haven't seen him in over a week. He's away on business again."

"Things getting any better between Owen and Jeremy?"

"Not really. My son is the most stubborn male I've ever met. He's not willing to give Owen much of a chance, but he knows I won't put up with his rudeness. Owen is being so patient. Timmy is nuts about Owen, luckily. At least he has one of my sons in his corner."

"Things getting serious between you two?" Jenny knew Izzy and Owen had been dating awhile, but had a brief breakup this winter, mostly due to Jeremy. She thought things were going better for them now.

"I don't know…" Izzy sighed. "It would probably go better if he'd ever be in town for more than a few days. He keeps saying he's going to work it out so he's here for a month or so, but something always comes up."

"I guess the shop will be busy this summer, too. You always keep crazy hours at your shop in the summertime with all the tourists coming to town." Jenny shook her head. "I don't know how you do it all. Run your shop, raise two young boys… and plan your friend's wedding."

Izzy laughed. "But planning the wedding is fun. The boys are… a handful. But I love having my own shop and don't really mind the long hours in the summer. I'm just glad for the business the tourists bring in."

"You going on anymore antique buying trips to stock up the store before the rush hits?" Jenny asked.

"I think I'm fine. I did a lot of that this winter."

"That's good, 'cause I know your summer gets nuts." Becky Lee glanced at her watch again. "I think everything should be ready. Let me just pop in the kitchen and check."

Jenny dropped Izzy off at her home and decided to drop by Greta's house and see Clay for a few minutes. They'd both been so busy they'd hardly seen each other for days. She pulled into the drive and saw Clay and his mother sitting on the front porch.

Clay pushed off the porch swing, loped down the steps, and over to her car. "Hey, beautiful." His eyes lit up and he flashed his just-for-her smile. "This is a nice surprise. I'd almost forgotten what you look like."

Jenny slipped out of the car and Clay enveloped her in a hug. She rested in his arms for a moment, letting all the stress of the day and the litany of to dos fade away. "Hm, I needed that hug."

"Always have one waiting for you. Tough day?"

"Just a long one."

"Did you get more wedding things sorted out with Bella and Becky Lee tonight?"

Jenny pulled away from the hug and took Clay's offered hand. "We did. I'm lucky to have both of them or we'd never get to have this wedding."

"That doesn't work for me, Jenns. I'm already counting the days until I can call you my wife." He reached down and brushed a kiss on her forehead.

"I'm ready for it to just happen, too. I thought it was all going to be so simple. A small wedding at Izzy's, the reception at Sylvia's. But there is so much to do, even for such a simple wedding. Plus, I have to keep reeling Izzy in. She has such big plans."

They climbed the steps to the porch, arm in arm. Greta came back outside with a tray of sweet tea and cookies. "I thought you two might like some tea."

"That sounds wonderful." Jenny sank onto the porch swing and Clay handed her an ice cold glass of sweet tea. He sat down beside her and slowly pushed the swing with one foot.

"I'm going to run inside and check on the girls. Make sure they've finished up their homework. Danielle was more interested in texting her friends than studying for her math test." Greta paused at the door and looked back. "Glad you stopped by. It will be nice when you live right next door with Clay and the girls. I'll miss having them here, but I know y'all want your own place. I'm so glad it worked out that you could buy the Franklin's place."

"I'm glad we could, too." Jenny smiled at the older woman who had been as much of a mom to her as her own mother. Maybe more. All those years she'd dated Clay when they'd been teens, Greta had always been there for her.

Her own mother had always been held back by the strict rule book and criticism her father enforced upon his household. In the last few months she and her mother had become closer though, and Jenny was tentatively building a real mother-daughter relationship with her.

Greta walked inside and within seconds Clay had tilted her head up. His lips found hers and pressed a deep kiss against her lips. A rumbly sound of satisfaction escaped him. "I think we need some time alone, Jenns. I miss you."

"I miss you too. Maybe we could have a date night?"

"How about a picnic down by the river? Alone. No kids."

Jenny smiled. That was their place. A clearing by the river behind Greta's place. "That sounds nice. Maybe this weekend?"

"I'm on call this weekend."

Jenny sighed. "Of course you are. Maybe one night

next week? Though I think I have a couple of meetings. I'll check my calendar."

Clay let out a deep sigh of frustration. "Well, the good thing about getting married, is at least I'll get to see you every night."

"And I'll get to see your face every morning."

Clay wrapped his arm around her shoulder. "Sometimes I can't believe how lucky we are to have found our way back to each other after all these years."

"We are very lucky." It had taken over sixteen years to find their way back to each other.

"And even though I missed Nathan's childhood, I'm very glad to have my son now."

"I'm sorry you missed those years, too. You know that. But I'm glad we have it all sorted out, that Nathan and I, and you and your girls, will soon be one happy family." She leaned her head on Clay's shoulder.

A swath of shimmering moonlight swept across the front yard and the stars danced up in the sky. A cool breeze began to swish the limbs on the trees, and she snuggled closer to Clay, absorbing his warmth. Jenny sat in silence with Clay, enjoying this perfect moment in contentment and peace.

A crashing sound came from inside the house.

"It's not my fault." Danielle's voice filtered from inside.

Clay sighed. "I should go in and see what's going on." He stood up and took Jenny's hands, pulling her gently from the swing.

"I should go now, anyway. I still have papers to grade before tomorrow."

Clay stuck his head in the door. "I'll be in in a minute. Don't break the house apart before I get there. Just need to walk Jenny to her car."

"Everything's under control." Greta called back.

Clay walked her across the uneven front yard and over to her car in the driveway. "Thanks for coming over." He leaned down and brushed a kiss against her lips. Her heart raced and she swallowed back the emotions rushing through her.

She climbed in the car and pulled out of the driveway. The image of Clay got smaller and smaller in her rear view mirror as she drove away. Just as she reached the end of the drive, she saw him turn and head back into the house.

Suddenly she felt alone and bereft, adrift in a sea of emotions. Must be all the wedding plans, the stress of moving, and the crazy schedule of the school year. But she couldn't shake the feeling that something wasn't right.

CHAPTER 4

Hunt sat outside the boys' school, waiting for the dismissal bell to ring. He was early, but didn't much care. It was a nice warm day. The sun was shining. He had a nice brick wall to sit on. The sun chased its rays through the magnolias in the school yard. A light breeze tickled the branches and they twitched slightly in response. He wished he'd thought to bring his camera, it would have made a great shot.

He used to always have at least his small mirrorless camera with him, but since he'd come home he'd pretty much given up that habit. He wasn't sure why though. It just seemed silly to be taking pictures here in Comfort Crossing. He was used to shooting drama, capturing traumas in the world. Sometimes the scenes he captured actually took his breath away with their horror or their realistic capture of a tragedy.

"Hey, you. You look lost in thought."

He glanced up and saw Keely standing beside him.

She had on, once again, a simple top, skirt, and some kind of sensible looking flat shoes. Her hair was pulled back into a twisted thingie on the back of her head. She must be headed to work. From what he'd seen, this was standard work attire for her.

"You caught me. I guess I was day dreaming."

"What were you dreaming about?"

"I was thinking that would make a good shot." Hunt nodded towards the schoolyard.

"So, why not take it?"

"Don't have my camera. Could grab a shot with my phone, I guess." Not that he considered phone pictures real photos. He admitted he was a self-proclaimed photo snob.

"I've rarely seen you without your camera. You always had one when we were in high school. Kind of annoying with it, actually." Keely grinned at him. Her face lit up for a moment, relaxed, carefree.

"I wasn't that bad, was I?"

"Let's see, you took that one picture of me at the homecoming game... what year was that? The one where it rained all through the game? I looked like a drowned rat. And you put it in the school newspaper."

"Well, okay. I did that." He smiled. He remembered he'd done that specifically to provoke Keely. And it had worked.

"There was that one of Katherine when she fell on her butt from the cheerleaders' pyramid. She was covered with mud."

"Okay, I'll admit to that one, too." He'd forgotten about all the crazy shots he'd taken of his friends.

"Then there was that one of Kevin. You caught him sneaking into the teacher's lounge to swipe a donut. The look on his face was priceless."

"Yes, that one. It was easy to get great shots of Kevin. He was always up to something." Hunt felt a pang of loss. It seemed to creep up on him from nowhere, just when he thought he had it all under control. He quickly tucked away the pain.

"You miss him, don't you?" Keely's voice was low and soothing. She'd never been one to just let things go. Which annoyed him and charmed him depending on whether she turned it on him.

"I do. Sometimes I almost forget he's gone. Something happens and I want to pick up the phone and call him. Instinct, I guess. It's kind of weird." That was more of his feelings than he'd shared with anyone for a long time. He wasn't sure what had made him tell Keely that now.

"I'm sorry. I know it's hard on you. And Natalie. I don't know how she deals with it and those three boys. That's a lot for one person. I'm glad you're back here helping her for a while."

"I'm not sure how much help I am. I mean, I can drive them and pick them up. Watch them a bit. But I don't really have a handle on this raising kids gig." He'd never been good at the responsibility thing. He'd tried before, oh how he'd tried. But he'd failed.

He wanted to feel like he was helping, but more often than not, Jackson looked at him like he was from another planet. Hunt was so not like Kevin. He was sure

Kevin was a natural born father, who knew instinctively what to say and what to do.

Keely leaned against the brick wall and dropped her purse on the ground. "I'm sure that's a big help and I bet she enjoys having another adult around to talk to."

"Yep, living the glamorous life, living on the back porch, pouring cereal for the boys. Big help."

"How long are you planning on staying?"

"I'm not sure." He wasn't certain how long he could stay. The rational part of him reminded him that he made his living traveling and taking his photos. What was there for him to do in Comfort Crossing?

"The back porch doesn't sound all that bad, though honestly, I think a place of your own would be the ultimate luxury. I'm still living at Mom's. I help with Katherine. It just never seemed the right time to move out. I'd so love to have my own place though."

"Why don't you look into it then?"

"I'm afraid Mom and Katherine would feel like I was deserting them. And Mom would go on about how she needs help with Katherine."

"Maybe Katherine needs to learn how to do more for herself."

"That's not fair. You have no idea, Hunt. She's had it so hard. Kat was so active before. She was going to graduate and run the restaurant. She loved working there."

"So, why doesn't she work there now?"

"Well, she can't."

"Why not?"

"Well, for starters, we'd have to revamp the whole

restaurant to make more room for her to wheel around, if she started hostessing. She can't carry the food out to waitress, and same problem with the space constraints. We did take out some tables so she can get through to the whole first row of tables, and back to the office area, and the kitchen. But there is only so much space available. We'd have to retrofit the whole kitchen lower if she were to work in the kitchen. Besides, cooking is so not her strong suit."

"Does she want to work there?"

"No. I don't think so." Keely paused. "Well, I never really asked her. She stopped working there after the accident. She had so many operations, then so much therapy. She never came back."

"What does she do all day?"

"Well, she went to college. That took a lot of years. She had to drop out a couple of times for more operations. Now that she graduated she reads a lot. Knits. She keeps busy."

"Is she happy doing that?"

"Happy?" Keely looked confused. "I guess so. She doesn't complain. She seems resigned to how the accident changed her life. It changed all our lives."

"I'm sure it did. Did they ever find out what really happened?"

"Not for sure. They think she just lost control of the car and hit that tree." A haunted look crossed Keely's face.

"No hope for her walking again?"

"No."

"I'm sorry, Keely. I know it really changed your life.

I thought you were all set to go away to the University of Missouri to journalism school."

"I was, but it's not like I could just leave and let Katherine deal with all of it on her own."

"She had your parents there to help her."

"Hunt, back off. She needed me."

"I'm sorry, I didn't mean to make you mad. You just had such big dreams."

"Yes, well real life got in the way of all of that." Keely's voice was flat and cold. She pushed off the wall. "I better go. The dinner shift will start soon."

He hadn't handled that conversation very well. He shouldn't have opened his big mouth. She obviously had a lot of responsibilities now. The cafe, her family. She used to be such a carefree girl. Nothing like this serious woman who walked away from him as if the weight of the world was carefully balanced on her shoulders.

After a week Keely was certain Natalie was the best thing that had happened to Magnolia Cafe in a very long time. She quickly dug right in and besides just waiting on her tables, she arrived early and helped set the tables up, refilled salt shakers and napkin holders. She frequently delivered orders for the other waitresses if they got backed up. She was always on time, always had a smile. She always seemed to know what needed to be done and did it without asking. It took such a load off of Keely's shoulders to have another dependable employee. Natalie also got along great with Becky Lee.

Things were running a little more smoothly now. Keely had hoped her mother would notice how well things were going, but if she had, she hadn't mentioned it.

Keely and Natalie sat at one of the tables after the lunch rush wrapping bundles of silverware in napkins. "Natalie, I'm not sure what I did without you."

"I'm glad to have the job. I need the money. I have to play it pretty tight these days. Anyway the tips are good and I enjoy the work."

"I'm glad it worked out for both of us." Keely glanced around the cafe. It basically looked about the same as it always had.

"What's wrong?" Natalie asked.

"What do you mean?"

"Well, you just gave a big sigh."

"I was looking around here. It just looks so much the same. I wish I could update the look some."

Natalie slowly walked around the Cafe. "You know, it wouldn't take too much to spruce the place up. Make it look more homey and less... well, I don't want to hurt your feelings, but less dated."

"That's exactly what I'd like. I just don't have a lot of spare cash to throw at it. And there is arguing with my mother about any changes."

"I got a lot of the things in my house from shopping the antique malls around the area. Bella's Vintage Shop has some great pieces. You could maybe get a big wooden hutch for over there in the corner to hold the menus, the silverware bundles, and the water pitchers. And you know what would look great there by the front window in the alcove where the customers wait? Replace those chairs all lined up, with a long old wooden church pew."

Keely squinted her eyes, trying to imagine the changes. "You know, that would look nice I bet." She grinned at Natalie. "Okay, what else?"

"Well, you really need more space for people to wait."

"I know that. Same problem. My mother."

Just then the bell over the door jangled and Hunt came inside. "Hi, ladies."

"I'm not quite ready to go, Hunt. Can I get you a cup of coffee while I finish up here?"

"That'd be fine. No hurry."

Keely saw her sister outside the cafe and jumped up to get the door for her.

"You know, Keely, I really can open the door on my own."

"I was just trying…"

"I know, trying to help."

Katherine wheeled past her and headed over to where Natalie and Hunt were sitting. Keely followed along behind her sister, mentally judging whether the tables were far enough apart in the corner for her sister to fit through. Though they'd taken out some tables after the accident, they'd missed the income from the extra tables. Her sister hadn't been coming around much lately, and Keely was embarrassed to admit she'd added a few more tables back in. They could sure use them on the weekends.

Keely followed her sister back to the table where she'd been sitting. "How did you get here?"

"I wheeled over." Katherine grinned. "Mother was driving me nuts. She finally went to take a nap and I left her a note."

"I would have come and gotten you."

"It's a pretty day. It's only a couple of blocks."

She didn't know what had gotten into her sister's head. And she was certain her mother would think this was all her fault, not her sister's, that somehow she'd made her do this.

"Hi, Natalie. Hunt, I haven't seen you in forever. How've you been?"

"Pretty good."

"So, what are you guys up to?"

"Natalie and I were actually talking about making some changes to the cafe."

"Really? Like what?" Katherine jumped in eagerly.

It had been a long time since Keely had seen Katherine interested in much outside of her existence at home. She had TV shows she watched, read books constantly, knit afghans and socks. As selfish as it sounded, Katherine kept her mother occupied so she wasn't constantly criticizing Keely, and that worked out just fine as far as Keely was concerned.

Keely and Natalie explained the changes they'd talked about. "But then we were just starting to discuss the problem with no room for people to wait for a table when it gets busy."

"So what about your idea to use the patio area out back? That would work for most of the year. Like you always said, Keely, if you had more seating, there would be less people waiting for a table."

When had Katherine started to pay attention to what she'd said about the cafe's business? Keely watched her sister's eyes light up with the discussion. Maybe she hadn't been giving her sister enough credit.

"Really, you have a patio out back?" Natalie set down the salt shaker she was filling.

"Yes, but it would need a roof put over it. Maybe some partial sides? And, of course, it can't cost much." Keely smiled weakly.

"Let's go take a look." Hunt pushed away from the table.

They all trailed out to the back of the restaurant and through the French doors to a very tired, small patio. The edges were covered in raggedy underbrush.

"Well, the good thing is the patio itself is in good shape. It could be enlarged a bit, too." Hunt paced off the patio.

"I think with a roof, some partial sides, and a bar at the far end, you could make it into a kind of wine garden out here." Natalie suggested.

Keely tilted her head and eyed the space. "I could see that. The customers could wait out here and have a drink. Or come out here after dinner and enjoy a glass of wine. This might work."

"Some ceiling fans to stir the breeze during the summer," Katherine added. "Some of those heater lamps for colder weather."

"Those are great ideas to extend the time we could use the area. I bet we could use it almost the entire year then. But, I'd still have to convince Mother. That might be the biggest hurdle. And finding someone to do the work at a reasonable price."

"I can help you with that" Hunt stopped tugging at some errant brush at the edge of the patio.

"What, convincing my mother, or finding someone to help build it?" Keely grinned.

"I'll help you convince Mother. Really, when is the last time you've heard her turn down anything I've asked for?" Katherine wheeled her chair to face Keely. "I might as well exploit it a bit."

It was sad, but true. Their mother did fall over herself to do whatever she thought Katherine wanted. Katherine never abused it, but it sure could be used to their advantage here.

Hunt walked over to the French doors and looked around. "So, since you have the convince-your-mother thing figured out, I meant help with converting this to a wine garden. I put myself through school doing construction. Honestly, it's the one thing I know how to do as well as shoot photos."

"I couldn't ask you to do that. You're a photographer, not a construction guy."

"I don't think you asked, I offered. And I need something to keep me busy while I'm here. I enjoy construction work."

"Are you sure?"

"Positive."

Natalie clapped her hands. "This is great. You'll be around more. We'll have to figure out some kind of arrangement with the boys though. On days I'm working, if you're working too... I have to figure something out."

"I could watch them." Katherine paused in her work.

"You can't do that." Keely stared at her sister.

CHAPTER 5

"W hy not?"

"Well, because. I mean…"

"A person in a wheelchair can't watch kids?" Katherine nailed her with a stare.

"I didn't mean that, I meant…"

"What did you mean?" Hunt joined in.

Great, she was going to get it from everyone. How could Katherine keep up with three active boys? Where would she watch them?

"If you're working the dinner shift, they could walk to our house after school. It's only a few blocks. I could get them a snack, help them with their homework. You could pick them up on your way home. I wouldn't charge much. I figure it would be like me contributing to the running of the cafe some."

"No, I'd have to pay you a fair wage."

"A low fair wage then."

"What about Mom?" Keely looked at her sister, still not convinced.

"What about her?"

"Oh, Keely is right. Your mom would probably go nuts with the boys and their energy level." Natalie shook her head.

"Well, the way I see it, we all need to start pulling more weight around here. Not just Keely. Mom and I do, too. I know Mom rarely comes into the cafe anymore. It's not fair to Keely to do everything. I'll talk Mom into it."

"Along with convincing her we need the patio fixed up and seating back there?"

"Yes, along with that. And while we're talking about changes, I'm going to start working at the cafe some, too. I'm great with bookwork, you can show me how to do some of it. Might as well put that college degree to work."

"Katherine, you can't take on so much at once."

"It's not at once. I've graduated. It's time I get a job. This will help out."

Keely could feel Hunt watching her. Seeing how she'd react to this. Judging her. He'd no idea how hard it was to shoulder all this responsibility. But Katherine hadn't worked a day in her life. She couldn't just jump in with two feet. Keely paused, realizing how outrageous her thoughts were. Two feet. As if.

"Okay, I give up. Natalie will usually have two dinner shifts. So you could watch her boys then. And I'll start showing you some of the bookwork."

"When?"

Keely looked at her sister, so eager to jump in and help. Where had this come from? She was so used to protecting her sister. Making things as easy as possible for her. She'd a rough enough life as it was.

"Well, first you talk to Mom and convince her you can watch the boys. And that fixing the patio is a good idea. Then we'll go from there."

"Oh, that's all I have to do." Katherine laughed. "I'll convince her. Just you wait and see."

Katherine didn't waste any time.

"Mother, this is something I want to do." Katherine sat across the table from their mother, a look of determination in her eyes.

Keely looked back and forth between her mother and Katherine, not sure who was going to win this time.

"You can't do that. It's too much."

"Which part? Watching Natalie's boys or working at the cafe?"

"Well, both. Three boys would be too much for even a... well, someone who could chase after them. And how would you get back and forth from the house to the cafe?"

"That's another thing I wanted to bring up, as long as we're talking about changes. I'm going to learn to drive and get my driver's license. I've looked into getting an old used car and getting hand controls. I'm tired of depending on others to get around everywhere."

"But... You can't."

Keely watched her mother sputter and her face turn bright red.

"Kat are you sure?" Keely rarely agreed with her mother, but maybe Kat was taking on way too much at once.

"I'm positive. I can't just sit around my whole life. I've been unsure about what I can do, but I think this is a good start. Mother, we've let Keely shoulder all the responsibility for the family for too long. I'm quite capable of helping her now. I'm going to have her show me how to work on the books. I've always been organized and good with numbers."

"Katherine, you just cannot take on all these new jobs at once. You'll get worn out. You just can't."

"Worn out like Keely is all the time?" Katherine looked over at her sister. "Haven't you noticed how exhausted she is? When is the last time you heard her laugh? When is the last time she's taken a day off work?"

Keely reeled from the tirade that was Katherine right now. She'd no idea her sister even noticed these things.

"We need to start pulling our own weight. It's not Keely's job to support all of us, to work the restaurant every day with no break."

Keely looked down when she felt Katherine take her hand. She squeezed her sister's hand, fighting against the tears that threatened to spill.

"You put her up to this, didn't you?" Their mother turned and pinned Keely with a steely stare. "You know she can't take on all of this. It's too much."

"This is not Keely's idea. She argued with me at first. But it's not Keely's decision or yours to make. I'm going to do these things. We've all been living on hold for years, I know. Ever since my accident. But it's time we moved on. Everything can't be about me and the accident. I've recovered as much as I'm going to. I went to college for goodness sake. I can certainly take care of the boys, work at the cafe, and learn to drive."

"Katherine, I don't think you're thinking rationally. Why don't you try just taking on one thing at a time? Do a bit of the bookwork. You can't do all of this."

"Ah, Mother, but I can. I'm ready to join the world again. I'm tired of hiding in this wheelchair letting life just whoosh by me."

"Oh, and one more thing." Katherine looked at their mother, her shoulders set in determination. "We're going to convert that old patio area behind the cafe and add in seating out there. Maybe a bar at the far end. A place for people to wait for their dinner or sit and have an after dinner drink."

Keely waited for her mother to explode. Instead, her mother got up from the table and looked at both of the sisters. "It's clear to me that you don't want my approval or need my help. Do whatever you want. Make your own mistakes. I've tried so very hard with you two girls. Done everything for you. And this is how you repay me. Fine. Do what you want."

Her mother's footsteps echoed down the hallway and ended with a firm almost-slam of her mother's bedroom door.

Katherine bit her lip, then grinned. "Well, that went well."

Keely broke into laughter and Katherine

immediately tried to shush her while holding in her own giggles.

"Oh, yes. That went down right smoothly."

"She's usually quicker at giving in to me." Katherine shook her head. "I guess I hit her with too much all at once."

"I guess you did." Keely smiled. It had been a long time since she'd felt so much like a sister. "How about we go to the cafe and have some pie and coffee. We'll make plans."

"That will give Mother time to come around to all of this."

"If you think so." Keely was doubtful her mother was ever going to agree with any of their plans. The problem was, what was her mother going to do to try to stop them?

Bella rushed down Main Street, the misty rain covering her in a cold dampness. She clutched her jacket closed as she hurried along. She stopped in front of the Magnolia Cafe and shook her head, spraying fine droplets from her curls. She shook her arms, trying to dry a bit before heading into the restaurant, not wanting to drip rain all over their entryway.

She pushed into the cafe and glanced around. Back in a corner table Keely, Katherine, Becky Lee, and Natalie sat at a table. They waved at her to have her come on back.

"Thanks for meeting with us." Keely held up a cup. "Coffee?"

"Yes, please."

Becky Lee scooted over to make room for Bella. "I told them you could help find a few pieces of furniture for the restaurant."

"I'd love to help. Tell me what you have in mind." Bella loved the challenge of finding just the right piece for her customers. She often had the furniture in her vintage shop already, or even more fun, would go out looking for them.

"Natalie had a couple good ideas. A church pew on the wall under the windows where people can sit and wait for a table." Keely then nodded towards a space on the wall by the kitchen. "And over there, maybe a big hutch to hold silverware, napkins, extra menus."

"And Keely is going to add a patio out back. We'll need tables and chairs out there. The patio will have a top over it, but the table and chairs will have to handle being outside," Natalie explained.

"But, we're trying to keep our expenses down as much as possible." Keely looked worried.

"You know, I saw the neatest tables at this cute little restaurant over in Bay St. Louis. I talked to the owner, who said she'd tried to cut back on all expenses possible when they reopened after the hurricane came through and wiped them out. Their tables were made of paneled and carved doors covered with polyurethane poured over them to make them flat. Hard to explain, but they looked wonderful and the owner said they stood up to a lot of abuse. They used random things for legs. Some wrought iron legs. Some thick spindles salvaged from a stairway. It looked really nice."

"I love that idea." Natalie's eyes lit up. "I bet we could get Hunt to help us make those."

"Gil has every woodworking tool known to mankind. I'm sure I could convince my brother to help." Bella took out a notebook. "I bet I could find the old doors for you for not much at all. I actually have a few in the back storeroom of the shop. Haven't had space to put them out yet. We could then do a mix of old chairs with them. Seal them up with weather coating. More funky eclectic than mismatched."

"We were thinking about a bar at the end of the area. Just to serve up wine and beer, nothing fancy, providing our liquor license goes through. I told Mother I thought it was time the cafe got a license. She wasn't happy, but most of the other restaurants in town serve alcohol. I think it will help us keep our business and expand, even." Katherine had out a notebook and was taking notes while they talked.

"Oh, I know where to find an old bar for you, too. I saw it at a store that was closing. It's an old wooden counter, but I think it would work perfectly."

"I have to keep the expenses down. We don't have much to work with. We still have the expense of converting the old patio and putting the roof up over it." Keely bit her bottom lip.

"How about I do some looking around and give you an estimate of what I think this would cost?" Bella jotted down some notes in her leather planner.

"Another notetaker, I see." Katherine smiled at her.

"If I don't write it down, it doesn't happen. It's the only way I can juggle so many things without something falling through the cracks. I do big notebooks for projects I work on."

"Y'all should see the notebook Izzy did for Jenny's wedding. It's a masterpiece." Becky Lee teased.

Bella grinned. "I do love me a pretty notebook."

"I'm hoping all this will bring in more business to the cafe. The patio with extra space. Updating the look of the cafe just a bit." Keely's eyes held a tinge of uncertainty.

Bella wasn't surprised that Keely was cautious. She was glad Keely was trying to improve the cafe and increase business and she felt an intense sisterhood with the woman trying to make a go with her business in this town. The struggles of owning a small business hit so close to home.

"You know, it's too bad we don't have a big beginning of summer festival. Like how the town has Festival Days at the end of the summer right when school starts up. If we had a big town event at the beginning of the summer, maybe we could attract more tourists right at the start of the season. It might carry through for a while." Katherine tilted her head to one side and tapped her pen on the table.

Keely sat up straight and set down her coffee cup with a clatter. "Kat, that is a really good idea. I mean like a great idea."

"It is. I'd love to bring in more tourists to town. That will help business at my shop, for sure." Bella really liked this idea. She liked it a lot. "We could try to get most of the business on Main Street and Rosewood Avenue involved. It would benefit everyone."

"We only have a few months to pull this off, though. We could do it over Memorial Weekend. School will have just let out for the kids." Katherine turned the page in her notebook and started scribbling notes.

"Remember when the town used to have parades. Why don't we do that anymore? They were so fun to watch when I was small. We could organize a parade. Maybe have an arts and crafts festival in the town park," Natalie chimed in.

Bella wrote that idea down, too. "These are great ideas. A Summerfest."

"Oh, that's a great name to call it." Katherine jotted some more notes.

"I think you and Katherine should be in charge of Summerfest." Becky Lee grinned. "I mean, you two already have the notebooks full of ideas."

"Oh, I don't know. Katherine has taken on so much in the last few weeks." Keely looked worried.

"Thanks for answering for me, sis." Katherine glared at Keely. "Actually, I'd love to help plan this. What do you say, Bella?"

"I'm in. I just need to make sure I can get Jenny's wedding pulled off the following weekend. But we have most of that planned out already." Bella had so many ideas racing through her mind. This was going to be great. Maybe it could become an annual thing if it worked out this year. She wrote down a few more notes.

Becky Lee laughed. "See, Izzy is never happier than when she's right in the middle of planning something."

Bella grinned at her friend. She might be right. She was at her happiest when she was busy planning an event. "It's settled then. Summerfest is on."

CHAPTER 6

K eely glanced out through the French doors at
Hunt working on the patio. He bent over and
tugged out some weeds at the edge and tossed them into
a growing pile near the edge. He was dressed in only a t-
shirt in the cool April weather, but he'd broken a sweat
at the exertion of clearing the space. He reached for a
small blue cloth tucked into the back pocket of his jeans
and swiped at his face. With a quick arch of his back
and a roll of his shoulders, he leaned back down and
attacked another weed.

Pulling those weeds out by hand had been his idea.
She would have gone the chemical route, but he'd
insisted he'd seen enough damage from chemical spills
around the globe. He'd pull the weeds then spray the
remainder with vinegar. She'd never heard of that, but
she'd given him free rein over the project. Hopefully that
wasn't a mistake. After days of talking, they'd decided he
would build a partial wall around the patio, after

enlarging the patio with new paving stones. He planned to build a roof over the area. If all this worked out, then eventually Keely was going to purchase roll down plastic window awnings that could be pulled down to keep out rain, or help keep in the heat during the winter.

Hunt had promised he'd have it finished by Summerfest. Keely was surprised he planned on staying that long, but he insisted he would be in town until then. She wasn't sure what he planned to do after that.

She stood there watching him for a bit. A tool belt slung low on his hips. The t-shirt stretching across his chest as he wrestled the weeds.

Hunt looked up and waved when he saw her standing in the doorway. A warm blush washed over her. Nice. Caught in the act of stalking him.

She opened the French door and peeked her head out. "The lunch crowd has wound down. Would you like to come in and join me for something to eat? I was just getting ready to take a break," Keely offered, hoping he'd no clue how long she'd been standing there staring at him.

"Let me try to get a bit more presentable. Don't want me chasing off your customers."

"You're fine." Keely though he actually looked more than fine.

He reached up and wiped his face with the blue towel, then stuffed part of it in his back pocket where it hung down like a flag. "I guess you could put me in the farthest corner of the cafe."

"Kind of like time out when you were a kid?" Keely smiled.

"So you remember, huh?"

"I remember all the way back to grade school. Miss Green's class. I think you spent more of the school day in the time-out corner than at your own desk."

"She just didn't like me. It wasn't my fault."

"I'll admit she was one of those teachers who liked the goody-two-shoes girls the most."

"Like you?"

"Hey, I ended up in the time-out corner once."

"Bet you were traumatized for life."

She looked up at him and it wasn't until she saw the wicked grin he flashed her direction that she realized he was teasing her.

"Well, I do remember very vividly to this day. It *was* traumatic. I wasn't the kind of student who got into trouble. The chair squeaked and I tried to sit very still so I wouldn't attract her wrath again. I hated how she had the desk set so your back was to the room. I thought everyone was pointing at me and talking about me."

"So what was your infraction?"

"I was passing a note to Bobby Riker. It wasn't even my note. It was that bossy Camille's note. I was too scared to say no to her."

Hunt tossed his head back and laughed. "I'd forgotten all about her. She was something, wasn't she?"

"I think she had it out for me. She was horrible to me all the way through high school. Not sure what I ever did to her except take her punishment for passing a note in grade school." Keely grinned.

"Wonder what ever happened to Princess Camille."

"I heard she moved to Mobile. I see her every once in a while in town. Visiting her mother, I guess."

"Does she still strike fear in your heart when you see her?" Hunt cocked an eyebrow.

"Would I admit that I crossed the street to the other side last time I saw her walking down the Main Street? Nope, I'd never admit that."

"Well, if we ever run into her, I promise to protect you." Hunt winked.

"Mighty nice of you, kind sir." Keely had forgotten how much fun she'd had joking around with Hunt when they were growing up. She'd better keep on her toes, she was so out of practice joking with someone that it had taken her a while to figure out he was teasing her.

Hunt took off the tool belt and set it on the ground. "I'll just pop in the restroom and clean up a bit."

Keely stood sideways in the doorway to let him pass and watched him walk over to the restroom. She kind of missed seeing the sexy tool belt slung low on his hips…

Hunt splashed water on his face and scrubbed up to his elbows. He snatched a paper towel from the dispenser and dried off as best he could. Hunger rumbled through him and he was glad Keely had suggested lunch. Sometimes when he got deep into a project he forgot to eat until he became a cranky bear. He was pretty sure Keely didn't want to see the cranky bear side of him.

He brushed some dirt off the leg of his jean. That's as good as it was going to get. He went out into the cafe and looked for Keely. She sat perched at the counter, sipping a glass of tea, waiting for him. With a few strides he crossed over and slipped onto the stool next to her.

"Starving." He reached for a menu. Not that he really needed it. Not much had changed since he'd been coming here as a boy.

"What do you want? I'll turn in our order."

He set the menu down. "I'll have a burger, fries, vanilla shake."

"We have fresh peach pie."

"And a piece of pie. With ice cream."

"Thought so." She got up from the stool, walked back to the kitchen, then came back out and busied herself making his shake. He watched while she added the ice cream to a large silver shaker and placed the container beneath the shake machine. She poured the shake into a large glass, squirted some whipped cream on it, then plopped a cherry on top of that.

"Here you go." She placed the drink in front of him along with a long handled spoon.

He took a sip. Just as good as he remembered. "That's great."

Keely crossed around the counter and perched on the stool next to him again. They sat in silence for a bit. He wondered what she was thinking as she stared off into space.

"Penny for your thoughts?" He set down his glass.

"What? Oh, I was thinking about all the changes here. Mom is barely speaking to me, she thinks everything is my fault. Katherine is taking on too much at once and I'm worried about her. Watching Natalie's boys, trying to learn the books here, and now working on Summerfest."

"She seems pretty happy doing all that. Maybe she wanted to take on more responsibility and not feel like she wasn't contributing."

Keely chewed her bottom lip. It mesmerized him. *No, it didn't.* He looked up to her eyes, instead. And that didn't help. Not one bit. He started to figure out just which shade of brown he'd call her eyes. Brown eyes didn't do them justice. They were tinted with honey highlights.

"What are you staring at?" Keely interrupted his thoughts.

He figured he wouldn't tell her about the mesmerizing lips, but would go with her eyes. "Sorry. Hazard of being a photographer. I'm always looking either at the light or colors. I was trying to come up with a good description of your eye color."

"Normal people would call them brown."

"So, you're saying I'm not normal?"

"Well, what did you come up with?"

"Whiskey colored," he said sheepishly.

"Ah. Well, that's the first time they've been called that."

Hunt picked up the shake and had another long sip of it, the cool glass soothing his chattering nerves. What is up with all this staring at Keely? They'd been friends forever. He snuck another sideways look at her while she drank her tea. She was good looking. She'd grown from tomboy, to gawky teen, to this accomplished-if-serious woman.

"You're staring again." Keely didn't even look up, but a blush tinted her cheeks.

"I'm sorry. It's that I just this very minute realized you're all grown up. Sometimes I still think of us as the kids we were in high school. Hanging out with Kevin. Going to parties. Worrying about passing the next exam."

She turned to face him then, staring right back at him. "We're not those kids any more though, are we? I have responsibilities. People counting on me. I can't just get up and gallivant all over the world."

Ouch. He sat back in surprise and it must have shown on his face.

"Oh, I'm sorry. That was harsh. I just meant… Well, I never had an opportunity to do all that traveling like I wanted. Didn't get to go to journalism school. First I needed to be here for Kat the year of the accident. It was all so horrible. My parents were so busy with her. Appointments. Surgeries. Therapy. I needed to pull my weight here at the cafe. Then my father died the next year and I had to take over running the place. I really had no choice."

Hunt didn't think she'd appreciate it if he told her he believed people always have choices so he kept that thought to himself.

"I'm sorry you had to take on so much, so young."

"I don't need your sympathy. It's just what I had to do." Keely's voice held a tenor of threat.

He needed to learn to keep his mouth shut around Keely. He was always mucking it up.

"Well, I admire all that you've done for your family."
Was that any better?

"We do what we have to do." Keely shrugged.

And sometimes you did what you had to do, and it wasn't enough.

"Keely, your order is up." The cook called from the doorway to the kitchen.

"I'll go get our lunch." Keely stood up and walked over to the kitchen.

He watched her walk away. The carefree girl turned overburdened woman. The set of her shoulders showed she was willing to bear the load.

But it didn't seem fair she had to do it alone.

Keely came back balancing their plates on a tray and set them down on the counter.

"Still starving?" Her face was flushed either from the heat in the kitchen or maybe a hint of embarrassment on revealing so much to him.

"You know what, Keely? I'm taking you out to dinner tomorrow night."

"What? I can't do that. The cafe is open."

"I'll talk to Natalie and Becky Lee. It's not a weekend night. And if Natalie can get her friend Sally to watch the kids, then Katherine could help out, too. I bet they'd all love to give you a night off."

"I couldn't."

As if an answer to his prayers, Becky Lee came walking into the cafe. "Hey, Becky Lee, got a second?" He waved her over to where they were sitting at the counter.

"You think Keely could have a night off tomorrow? I know Natalie is working."

"I think that's a fabulous idea. I'm working. We can cover it." Becky Lee's eyes lit up. "A night off for Keely. Never thought I'd see it happen."

"I haven't agreed to it." Keely looked at both of them like they were crazy.

"I'm taking her out. Dinner. Maybe a movie. We're going to have fun." Hunt gave Keely his best don't-argue-I'm-serious look.

"You should go." Becky Lee was taking his side, too.

"Okay. I give up. If Natalie can find childcare so Katherine can help, I'll go. Maybe mother will come in and help, too. Though I doubt it. She's barely speaking to either Kat or me right now."

Hunt pulled out his cell phone and dialed his sister. "Hey. Can you get a sitter for the boys tomorrow night so Katherine can work at the cafe? I'm going to take Keely out." He grinned at his sister's reply, glad Keely couldn't hear it. "Okay. Thanks."

He slipped the phone back in his pocket and turned to Keely. "All set. No more excuses."

"I don't know…" She bit her lip in that totally tantalizing way again then sighed. "Okay. I can't argue with all of you. I'll go."

"Your lack of enthusiasm is a bit hard on my ego, kiddo."

"No, I'm sure it will be fun."

But he wasn't hearing much assurance in her voice.

CHAPTER 7

K eely stood in front of the mirror and held up two dresses, totally undecided on what she should wear on a date. She hadn't been on a date in forever—or longer than that. And technically it wasn't a date. *Right?* She was just going to dinner, and maybe a movie, with a long-time friend.

So, what should she wear on this non-date? She sighed and looked in the mirror again. Most of her closet was skirts and sensible tops to go with them. Her standard attire for working at the cafe. She wanted to look different for a date. *No, non-date.*

"Hey, Keely. I know you're up there trying to decide what to wear. Bring down your choices and let me help you decide," Katherine called up the stairs.

A flash of distant memories danced through her mind. Kat standing in her room asking for advice on what to wear on a date with her boy-of-the-month.

She'd always been dating someone in high school. Well, until the accident.

Keely scooped up her three favorite choices and went downstairs to show her sister.

"Not that one. Too boring."

First choice nixed.

"That one makes you look like a librarian." Kat shook her head.

Second choice down.

"That one is okay, but come in my room. I have the perfect scarf to go with it to perk it up a bit. Oh, and how about some dangly earrings?"

She went to her sister's room and got loaded up with the scarf, earrings, and a bracelet Kat insisted she wear.

"Now, go upstairs and get ready, but come down here and let me do your hair for you. You're going to wear it down, and I'm going to curl it for you."

"I was just going to French braid it."

"Nope. Wearing it down. Trust me on this."

"Kat, you're making quite a fuss over all this."

"It's not every night that my sister goes on a date."

"It's not a date. I'm just going out to dinner with Hunt."

"Whatever you say." Kat's eyes twinkled with skepticism.

Their mother walked into the bedroom, eyeing the girls. "Are you sure you should leave Kat alone at the cafe?"

"Mother, I won't be alone. Becky Lee and Natalie will be there."

"I still say that's too much for Katherine. What if

something goes wrong?" Her mother stood in the doorway, one hand perched on her hip, a knee-quavering-guilt-inducing look on her face.

Katherine turned to Keely. "Don't. Don't even think about it. You're going."

"But, I—."

"Don't argue with me. Go finish getting ready." Surprisingly, Katherine could be almost as tough as their mother.

"Humph." Keely turned and walked past her mother. The disapproval she saw in her mother's eyes wasn't something new, but it hurt, just the same. She knew that look so well. Just once she'd like to see her mother's eyes shine with pride and approval.

She trudged up the stairs, the excitement of going on a date dampened by her mother's displeasure.

An hour later she was dressed, her hair was down and curled, and she'd dropped Katherine off at the cafe. Her mother had disappeared into her room with the almost door slam she'd perfected to a fine art.

Keely sat on the very edge of the worn sofa, waiting for Hunt. Her stomach did a cartwheel when she heard him pull into the drive. A totally inappropriate reaction for a non-date.

She got up, smoothed an imaginary wrinkle from her dress, then answered his knock at the door. He slowly looked at her from the top of her head to her almost-like-new heels. Low heels, but heels nonetheless. The look of approval in his eyes was unmistakable and chased after a thrill tumbling through her.

"You look great."

"Um, thanks." She shifted in the doorway to give him room to come inside. "You look good, too."

Hunt was dressed in khaki slacks and a blue, button-down shirt. His hair was still slightly damp from his shower. The light stubble beard he'd been sporting the last few days was gone. He brushed past her and walked inside.

"You about ready to go?"

"I am."

"I thought we'd go to Sylvia's Place. How does that sound? Or is there some kind of competition between you two for customers, and we should go somewhere else? I don't know the politics of all of this."

"No, Sylvia's Place sounds great. I've been wanting to try it out. It's fancier than the cafe. A different experience. More of a date place than a grab a bite to eat place." *Had she said date?*

Hm, Keely had said date place. So she considered this a date? He'd been afraid if he called it a date it would scare her off, which was the last thing in the world he wanted to do. 'Cause, for real, he wanted it to be a date.

Keely grabbed a sweater and her purse. He opened the door and they went out to the truck. He and Natalie shared her truck while he was in town. Becky Lee had promised to drive Natalie home after the cafe closed tonight so the shared vehicle situation was under control. He really should consider getting his own car, but that seemed silly since he didn't know how much longer he would even be here. He liked being here and helping out his sister, but it was a fine line he walked. He didn't want her to come to rely on him because they'd both seen firsthand what happened when he was put in the responsibility position. Well, he'd seen even more than Natalie. She hadn't seen his biggest failure. The one that still haunted him.

The truck growled to life and they were soon at Sylvia's Place, seated at a table by the window. Sylvia's son, Jake, had given them their menus and said he'd send their waitress over. They'd both ordered a glass of wine.

"It's nice that Sylvia and Jake could open this restaurant again. It's been in their family for so long."

"You don't mind the competition?"

"Not really. We don't have a lot of choices of places to eat here in town. With the growth of tourists coming in, we need places to eat, and places to stay."

"You think Bella and Katherine are going to pull off this Summerfest idea?"

"They both certainly seem organized enough, that's for sure. And Katherine is really determined to… I don't know, prove something? But I worry that she's overdoing it."

"I'll have to offer to help them."

"That would be nice. I'm sure they can use all the help we can give them. Kat said they'd already gotten quite a few of the town merchants to participate. Sales. Donations for advertising. Things like that." Keely paused while their waitress put down their wine glasses on the white linen tablecloth.

"Sounds like things are going well at this stage, then."

"They also talked to Rebecca at Sweet Tea B&B and told her the dates. I'm sure her B&B will fill up quickly. They talked to the two plantations outside of town that are now boutique hotels, so they would know the dates, too."

"Natalie said there was going to be a parade? I remember going to the town parade when I was a kid."

"They don't have that all worked out, but they do want to have one. I think they were going to talk to the high school band director to see if the band would play for the parade."

Their waitress came to take their order. They ordered their meals then settled back to enjoy their wine. He watched as Keely looked around the restaurant. He could tell her mind was racing, taking it all in. She ran her fingers lightly across the tablecloth.

"Comparing this to the cafe?"

She smiled sheepishly. "I can't help it. The white tablecloths... but I can't help but think of the laundry bill. Nice wine glasses. Waitresses and waiters in black pants and white shirts. And the wine menu. Oh, my gosh. The choices."

"So this was a good or a bad thing that I brought you here?"

"A good thing. I like seeing how Sylvia has things set up. I'm hoping our changes to the cafe will help bring in more customers and upgrade the place a bit, without losing its homeyness. I think that's what brings people to the cafe. It's familiar. You can come as you are, no need to get dressed up. You can come for a meal, or just a cup of coffee, or maybe a piece of pie."

"That is the strong point of your cafe. I think the patio in the back will be a big selling factor, too. If I ever get rid of those darn weeds." Hunt smiled.

Keely laughed. "You're getting closer to having it all cleared out so you can start on adding to the patio, aren't you?"

"Pretty soon. The brick pavers are ordered and should be in this week. I have part of the new area dug out and almost level. Need to get the sand in and packed down."

"I can't wait until it gets finished and we can open up the patio area."

"Did your mother ever jump on the bandwagon and agree it's a good idea?"

"Not at all. She's just pretty upset about everything right now. The patio. Kat working. Summerfest. You name it, she's dismayed about it."

"I'm sorry, that must be hard on you."

Keely's eyes flashed with… something… what was that look? A plea not to feel sorry for her? Appreciation that someone cared that things were hard on her? He held his breath, afraid he'd said the wrong thing yet again.

"Thanks. It is hard. It's always hard with Mother. She wants everything like it used to be with Kat walking and Father alive." Keely looked down at her wine glass and slowly twirled it in place. "Not that I really blame her. I wish I could whisk us back in time, myself."

"You would have gone on to journalism school, wouldn't you?"

Keely sighed. "There's really no use in talking about the what ifs, the if onlys. I don't want to get trapped into the habit my Mother has of trying to live in the past."

"It's too bad she fights you on all your decisions."

"Well, I used to let her have the final say on everything, but now with Kat wanting the patio too, I'm trying to stand up to her negativity and do what I think is best for the cafe. She's still the owner though. She could conceivably pull the plug on everything."

"Do you think she would do that?"

"I don't think so. Not with Kat on my side." Keely stared at her wine glass, lost in thought.

What a fine mess that would be if Keely's mom made her stop the construction of the patio. Or refused the purchase of the new furniture pieces for the cafe. Keely would be crushed. She was trying so hard to bring in new business to the cafe. Put her own spin on it. He couldn't imagine someone else having that much control over his life and over his decisions.

The waitress came and delivered their meals, interrupting both of them from their thoughts.

"It's really nice out tonight." Keely stepped outside the door to Sylvia's Place and looked down Main Street. A few other people walked down the sidewalks. The streetlights cast warm light along the street. "I think we can almost call it springtime."

"It is a nice night." Hunt stepped outside and stood next to Keely. She just reached up to about his chin. Her hair was down tonight, with curls drifting about her shoulders. He hadn't seen her hair down like that since their high school days. "Your hair looks good like that."

"Thanks. I usually just pull it back every day. Keeps it out of the way at work. But Kat... well, she insisted." She reached up and touched the curls self-consciously.

"Well, it looks really nice." *Really nice.* He cleared his throat. "We could look up and see what's playing at the movie theater."

"I don't know. You want to just walk for a bit? Enjoy the weather and the quiet?"

"Sounds good to me." He'd much rather take a walk and talk with Keely than sit in some movie theater. He crossed to the outside of the sidewalk and linked his arm through hers. "Let's go walk to the park."

They slowly strolled down Main Street to the town park, pausing occasionally to look in a store window and comment on something. Her eyes lit up at a teal dress in the dress shop window. "That would look great on you."

"Oh, I don't have a need for something like that. It is pretty, though."

"I guess you don't buy yourself many things that aren't needs, huh?"

"Just my journals. I buy really nice journals to write in every day."

"You do? What do you write about?"

She looked at him for a moment then took his arm

and started walking again. "I write about my day. My frustrations. Things I'm grateful for. I try to list off three things I'm grateful for every night before I go to bed. Helps me with my attitude."

"That sounds like a good way to end your day."

"I use my journals more for my thoughts. Not like Kat and Bella use their notebooks. They are all about plans." She looked up at him and smiled. "It's my one indulgence. I have a stash of nice notebooks. Leather ones or cloth ones covered in pretty floral fabric. Rich, thick paper in them. And fountain pens. With really nice ink. Kind of a frivolous expenditure, I could just as well write my thoughts in a dime store spiral notebook."

"Do you ever write articles or stories anymore?"

"Who would I write articles for? And I don't have time to write stories. All my time goes into making sure the cafe stays afloat."

"You're a great writer. I bet you could write for some of the regional magazines. Or your stories you used to write. They were really good."

Keely shook her head. "I just don't see where I'd find the time."

He figured he'd better drop the subject before he said the wrong thing. They crossed Main Street to the park and walked towards the gazebo. White twinkling lights illuminated the octagonal structure and spilled out into the park.

"It looks kind of magical, doesn't it?" Keely stood in front of the white painted gazebo, lined with benches on the inside, and the outside lined with magnolia bushes.

"It does a bit." He looked at it for a moment,

thinking in his head how he could capture it with his camera. The lights. The peacefulness. The small-town park, a safe place to walk in at night. How many people had that in their lives?

He dropped to the steps and Keely sat beside him. He wrapped his arm around her lightly and she leaned against him. They waved at the occasional passerby.

Keely rested a hand on his knee. "Do you miss traveling?"

"What? Well, a bit. But I'm going to stay here for a while until Natalie gets her feet under her." He was actually surprised he hadn't begun to feel restless yet. He usually got the urge to move on after a week or so in one place.

"How long do you think you'll stay?"

"I don't know. At least until after Summerfest."

Keely looked at him, her eyes a bit sad. A wistful looked crossed her face, and she turned and stared out into the night. "It must be so nice to be able to go away. Travel. See the world."

He didn't know how to answer that. Because it was nice. He loved the freedom to go where he wanted. Choose which assignment to take next. He'd wiped the dust of Comfort Crossing from his shoes when he'd left after high school, burying his failures. He was embarrassed how few times he'd actually come back to visit Natalie and the boys. Besides them, he really had no reason to return.

Except right then when he looked into those honey-brown eyes of Keely's and got lost in them. He could definitely think of a reason to visit more often. Before he knew what he was doing, before he could stop himself with all the reasons he shouldn't, he leaned down and kissed her. He reached a hand behind her head and cradled it, pulling her closer against his lips, deepening the kiss. Her hand reached around and rested on the back of his neck, warm, accepting, holding him close.

She sighed.

Then she quickly pulled away. "I... I mean... I'm sorry."

"Sorry you kissed me, or sorry you stopped?" He ran his knuckles gently along her jaw line.

She reached her hands up and shoved her hair away from her face. "I don't know what I mean."

He leaned down and kissed her again. Her breath came out in small wisps and she once again wrapped her arm around his neck. He stood up, pulling her with him and wrapped both his arms firmly around her small waist, pulling her close.

When he finally let her go, she clung to the sleeves of his shirt, looking lost.

"I should have done that years ago. Darn. Who knew?" There were definitely sparks there. He knew she felt them, too.

"I guess you should take me home now." Her voice was low and shook slightly with each word.

He paused and looked at her, afraid he'd scared her off.

She tossed him a weak smile. "It's getting late and I still have bookwork to finish before I go to sleep."

He had no idea if he'd done the wrong thing. If he'd

frightened her off. If she maybe thought he was nuts. *He was nuts.*

He looked at her, unable to read her. Unsure. "Okay. Home it is." He took her hand in his and led the way down the sidewalk in the park and out onto the cheerfully lit Main Street.

CHAPTER 8

N atalie went into Bella's Vintage Shop, eager to see some of the pieces Bella had talked about for the cafe. Keely had turned over the picking out of new furniture for the cafe to Natalie and she didn't take this responsibility lightly. She was glad to be able to help out Keely. Once they got an estimate of cost, they'd make the final decisions.

Bella led the way towards a room in the back of the shop. "This is the hutch I was thinking you could use for a server, menu holder, extra silverware rolls, etc. You could even put some extra salt and pepper shakers or whatever up in that top cabinet. If we finish the server part here, you could set pitchers of water or tea here."

"That looks fabulous. It's in pretty good shape, too. I bet Hunt would sand it down for us, and I could refinish it. Shouldn't take much time."

"Okay, I'll write down the price." Bella added it to a page in her notebook. "We'll look at things, make a

85

decision, then add things up and see what we come up with. I showed Keely a photo of the counter I found and she liked it, so I had it delivered here. If she doesn't want it, I'm sure I can sell it quickly. I have it in my store room. Come on back."

Natalie followed Bella through two more rooms in the old Victorian house Bella had converted into her shop. She kept getting sidetracked by the beautiful antiques and displays Bella had set up in the different areas of the rooms.

Bella's laugh filtered back into the room where Natalie was looking at a gate-legged table. "You coming? It's hard to walk by some of these pretty pieces, isn't it?"

"I'll say." Natalie hurried to catch up with Bella. "I can't imagine being surrounded by this every day. Setting up your displays. Going on trips to find new pieces. What a dream job."

"I do pinch myself sometimes. It's a lot of work, but I love it. I love the hunt for a nice antique at a good price. I love to refinish the pieces if they need it. When I moved my shop to this location, I finally had a room where I could spread out and refinish some of the pieces." Bella pushed open a door and flipped on a light.

Natalie looked around the room like a kid in a candy store. An old wardrobe was open and in the process of being painted a lovely teal color. Some old dresser drawers had spindle legs put under them to make tables and Bella had painted them in cheerful shades of green. "My goodness, Bella. You are so talented and clever. Look at these pieces."

Bella blushed. "Thank you. I do love fixing up the pieces I find."

"Those tables made out of old drawers are so cute."

"Sometimes I can salvage some old drawers out of furniture that is just too worn or broken to still use as a dresser. Or I take out the bottom drawers of a dresser and open up that area and make a television stand with space to put TV receivers or game consoles in that area. Then I use the drawers to make a table. I found a haul of old spindle legs I've been using." Bella crossed the room to the far corner. "Here is the counter I was talking about. I think it would work out perfectly for the bar. I got it for a steal."

"It has so much character. It will be perfect."

"I thought so."

"Here are some of the old doors I found at a thrift store. See this one? I've already poured polyurethane on top of it and it filled in the dips of the panels and now it's all flat."

"Oh, that looks nice. It will be a nice eclectic mix for the tables with the different doors."

"I thought I'd cut a few of them in half to make smaller tables, too."

"I should get Hunt to pick these up and we could put them out in the old garage behind my house. I'll help him work on them to get them all ready to go."

"I'll come help you when you start and show you how to do it."

"That would be great." Natalie walked over to a long wall lined with wooden chairs. "Are these the ones you've picked out for the patio?"

"Some of them. I also found a place that has a dozen chairs for sale for a really great price. I'm going to go run look at them in the next few days." Bella wrote down another note.

"So far, I think I'm actually going to come in a bit under Keely's budget. And it will be good publicity for my shop if people comment on the updated look at the cafe. Keely said she was going to promote my shop and tell everyone where the new pieces came from."

Bella showed Natalie the numbers and the estimate for the rest of the chairs and doors. "That's a really good deal you're giving Keely."

"I'm still making a fair enough profit, and the cross promotion will do me good." Bella grinned. "Besides I go there at least once a week. It will be nice to have the patio there and the inside updated a bit."

"I'm going to snap a few photos on my phone and show Keely, but she said she trusts me to pick out things more than she trusts herself."

"Just let me know. And if Hunt wants to come by and pick up the doors, he can anytime."

"I appreciate your help with all this. I want it to look so nice for Keely since she's kind of entrusted me with the redecorating."

"I think it's going to look great."

Natalie followed Bella out of the storeroom and back into the shop. She tried to resist stopping to look at each and every display Bella had put up. She needed to get back to the cafe and let Keely know what she'd found. Hopefully, with an okay from Keely, they could get started turning the doors into tables.

Natalie left Bella's shop and climbed into the truck. After Kevin had died she'd gotten rid of her car. She didn't need two vehicles and the truck had been all paid off. She liked driving Kevin's truck, it kept her feeling close to him. She hoped she had lots and lots of years left driving it. She pulled out of the parking space and headed over to the cafe. Hunt had said he wanted to use the truck this afternoon to pick up supplies for the patio.

~

"Hey, I'm home" Hunt walked in the door to his sister's house, set down his toolbox, and dropped his tool belt on top of it.

"Back here," Natalie called out.

Hunt walked to the front room and saw Natalie sprawled out on the couch. She looked exhausted.

"Bad day?"

"You could say that." Natalie tossed a pillow at him. "It was a crazy day at the cafe. One of the part-time waitresses quit again. And I managed to drop an entire pitcher of water."

"Sounds like a banner day to me." Hunt walked over where his sister was stretched out on the couch. He scooted her feet over and squeezed onto the end of the couch.

"Make room for me, sis."

"So, you had a bad day, too?"

"I had one heck of a day. I drove into Mobile to pick up the pavers for the patio. You know the ones that were supposed to be delivered that never were. So I went to pick them up myself and they only had half of the order. I don't know how I can finish the patio if I can't get the pavers. They aren't sure they can find enough to match what we already have."

"Do you think you'll get everything finished before Summerfest?" Natalie sat up on the couch and looked at her brother.

"I'd better because I promised Keely I would." *See what happens when people depend on him? Why do they do that?*

Hunt leaned back against the couch and put his feet on the old trunk his sister used as a feet-allowed coffee table. "Where are the boys?"

"Sally Hansen invited them over for dinner and a movie."

"That's a nice break for you."

"It might be a nice break, but now I feel obligated to have her three boys over one evening." Natalie sighed. "I don't know where I will find the time or the energy to reciprocate."

"I can help you with that, you can't do everything on your own." *Not that she should be depending on him, either.*

"You're doing enough to help me as it is." Natalie leaned forward and stretched. "I'm starving. I'm going to make a sandwich, you want one? I've got some leftover meatloaf."

"Sounds good."

Natalie went to the kitchen and he could hear her rattling around in there. He was tired but restless, and stood to wander around the room. He stopped by the bookshelf and ran his finger along the titles. The yearbook from the year he and Kevin had graduated caught his eye. He pulled it from the shelf and slowly opened it, not knowing if he really wanted to see the memories it held. A piece of paper fell out of the book and he leaned over to pick it up.

Kevin's handwriting. He still recognized it. He started reading the note before he even realized it must be for his sister.

Natalie came into the room right at the moment. "What are you doing?" Her eyes were wide in alarm.

"I just pulled out the yearbook to look at it. This note fell out. I'm sorry… I guess it's for you."

"I know what it is. Give it to me." Natalie put down the tray of sandwiches and held out her hand. "You had no business reading that."

"I just started reading, I didn't know…"

Natalie's voice got quiet. "He didn't want anyone to know. He wrote that note when he got sick, I guess he thought I'd find it after he was gone. But I found it before… before he died. So we talked about it, but he made me promise to never, ever tell anyone."

"He kept that secret all these years?"

"Yes, and he asked me to try to help out the Grangers as much as I could."

"Okay, explain to me exactly what happened."

"Katherine's accident was Kevin's fault." Natalie's words came out slow and her voice held such pain. "Kevin said he was out driving that night, coming home late from work. He started to fall asleep at the wheel and swerved into the other lane. He saw a car veer to miss him, but when he looked in his rear view mirror, he thought the other car was okay. He drove on home and went to bed. The next day he left to go to Maine for the summer to stay with his uncle. When he got back, he heard about the accident. Katherine was in the hospital with something like her third surgery."

"He's sure it was her?"

"He said it was a blue car. Her dad's car was that old blue Chevy, remember? It was totaled in the accident."

"I remember after the accident Keely gave her father the car she'd saved up all through high school to buy and take with her to college."

"Kevin never said a word to anyone but of course he blamed himself. I realized, after we talked, that's why he was always helping out at the cafe. Fixing things for them. I thought he just felt sorry for them after Keely's father died. I guess it was his way to help pay back for what he'd caused."

"He never said a word to me." Hunt sat musing. He thought Kevin told him everything. They'd been best friends back then. He remembered how Kevin had changed that fall, became more serious.

"I think it ate on him all the time. I would sometimes see this haunted look in his eyes when he thought I wasn't watching. He did become a different person after that summer. I thought he'd just grown up. But I think the whole ordeal made him become the super responsible person he became. I even think—though I know he loved me—that he married me out of some weird sense of responsibility to you. You were leaving to travel the world, and I was here alone. He wanted to take care of me for you." Natalie snatched a tissue and dabbed at the tears that slowly rolled down her cheek.

"Kevin loved you."

"I know he did. I do. But I think part of it was again, paying for his sins."

"You can't think like that, sis. I know he was nuts about you."

Natalie grabbed another tissue. "It's all so twisted now, though. I'll always have these doubts."

Hunt squeezed her hand. "You shouldn't. I know you made him happy. And he was a great dad. He loved being a dad."

"He was. He loved his boys. He felt so guilty when he realized he wouldn't be around to help raise them, to see them grow up."

"It must have been very hard on him."

"I think he felt like he was getting punished for his part in the accident."

Hunt reached up and rubbed the muscles in his neck. "I wish I would have been here for him. Could have talked to him. The poor guy."

He was Kevin's best friend, and he hadn't been there for him. Add that to the list of responsibilities he'd miserably failed.

"He made me swear I'd never tell his secret. You can't tell anyone. He was so ashamed of what he did, and so ashamed he never claimed responsibility when he came back. But at the end, he didn't want to be remembered as the man who caused Katherine's accident. Didn't want that for the boys. He never wanted the boys to find out. Ever."

"I won't, I promise."

"So, you see why I wanted to work at the cafe and help out Keely? For Kevin. But, it ends up I really do love working there. I like getting out of the house and talking to people. I like hearing the town news. I really like working with Keely and Becky Lee… and you know the silly thing? I feel guilty for enjoying the job. Like I'm not helping Kevin out since I'm enjoying it so much."

"You're a bit of an over thinker, aren't you, sis?"

"A bit. But I can't help it." Natalie shook her head. "I was so glad when you offered to help Keely and Katherine with the patio. I feel like we owe that family so much. They've been through a lot, it's the least we can do. For Kevin's sake."

Hunt grabbed an ice-cold beer out of the fridge and went out to sit on the porch. The night was cool enough that he'd had to pull on a sweatshirt. He sat on the porch swing and watched the moon climb higher in the star lit sky. The moon cast dancing tree shadows spilling across the yard. For a moment he considered going back in and grabbing his camera, but he didn't want to disturb Natalie. She'd fallen asleep on the couch in exhaustion from the day or from the trauma of telling Kevin's secret, or more likely, both.

Kevin. He couldn't get him out of his mind. He should have been here for his friend. Helped him deal with everything. At the very least he could have eased his mind with promises to help out Katherine and her family.

A cloud chased the moon in a game of tag, and the front yard was swallowed in darkness. Hunt took a long swallow of beer and stared out into the night, not really seeing anything, lost in thought.

"Hunt?"

He looked up. Keely stood on the top porch stair, one hand on the railing. The moon ran out from behind the cloud at that very moment and the moonlight drifted around her shoulders like a blanket, wrapping her in an unearthly glow.

Kevin. He looked up at the stars and almost nodded. *I got this one, buddy. Don't worry about a thing. I hear you.*

"Hey, Keely. What's up?" He kept his voice low. Afraid to break the spell he was under, or whatever it was. A chill ran up his spine.

"I was walking home and I thought I'd come home by way of Natalie's house. I was wondering if you had any luck getting the pavers today."

"I got some of them. Enough to get started. Don't worry about it, I'll get the rest." There was no way he was telling her there was a possibility that he couldn't find matching pavers. He would scour the whole country if need be. He'd cross that bridge when he came to it. *Cross that bridge when he came to it?* That wasn't his thought, wasn't something he said. But it *was* a phrase Kevin used to use. A lot. A shiver ran through him.

"You want to sit down?" Hunt slid over to the side

of the swing and motioned to the empty spot beside him. *Please sit down. Talk to me. Convince me I'm sane.*

"I could for a few minutes. I really should get home soon, though." Keely crossed the wooden porch, her footsteps echoing hollowly against the boards.

She sat down beside him on the swing and a cloud swept in front of the moon again, plunging them into semi-darkness, lit only by the light drifting out between the curtains on the front window. He could feel her warmth up against him, familiar and friendly, yet unnerving. He absentmindedly rocked the swing with one stretched out foot. She sat quietly, chewing on her bottom lip. The sign he now knew meant she was thinking.

"Something wrong?"

"I'm just worried about everything. Tired, too, I guess. Sometimes everything just overwhelms me. What if it gets too much for Katherine? What if I can't get more business for the cafe? How can I make enough to secure the future for not only me, but for Mother and Katherine?"

"That's a lot to worry about."

"Sometimes I wonder what life would have been like…" She turned her head away from him.

He reached over lightly touched her chin, bringing her back to face him. "What it would have been like if…?"

Keely looked straight into his eyes, then looked away again, staring out into the yard. "If Katherine hadn't had her accident. If I could have gone on to journalism school. If my father hadn't died." She sighed. "But what's the use of wondering? Life is what it is. We're all dealt our hands and have to live with it."

"I remember when we were kids we planned to travel the world together."

"I was going to be a famous journalist, winning international acclaim, while you took award-winning photographs. We were going to be free to go wherever we wanted. It sounded like heaven to me." Keely shook her head. "But, instead I'm destined to live out my life here in Comfort Crossing, running a cafe."

"Can't you try to change something? We all have choices."

"I don't. I've never had any choice. I had to take over the cafe, take care of Katherine and Mother." Her voice bristled.

"Have you asked your mother for more help? Or could you maybe try taking some classes? I'm pretty sure Loyola has a writing program. Can't you try to do some things for yourself, instead of always doing for others? You're going to burn out."

Keely turned back to look at him. "I am burned out. I've been burned out for years. But it doesn't matter. How in the world would I find time in my life to take writing classes? I can barely breathe now. Plus, now we're doing all these renovations on the cafe and add in plans for Summerfest."

"Katherine wants to help you, you know."

"She's doing enough as it is. I can't let her get worn down. It's not good for her."

"I think she's stronger than you give her credit for."

"Hunt, I know you're trying to help, but honestly, you don't have a clue."

Keely's eyes flashed with anger or impatience or aggravation—he wasn't sure which.

She cleared her throat and her voice dropped to almost a whisper. "Besides the whole thing is my fault."

The moon burst out of the cloud, flooding them with light and to his horror, tears were rolling down Keely's face. *Wasn't this his lucky day? He'd made two women cry in one night.*

"What's wrong?" Hunt reached over, took Keely's hand, and brought it close to his chest.

"Everything is wrong. And the last time I tried to take some writing classes? It got my father killed. So I don't think I'll be trying that anytime soon." Keely's voice was an aching whisper.

"What are you talking about?"

"About a year after Katherine's accident, I thought maybe I could do a little something for myself. Go into New Orleans a few nights a week and take a class. Start working slowly toward my degree." Keely pulled her hand away from his and sat staring at her hands folded in her lap.

Hunt stayed quiet, letting Keely tell her story in her own time. The chain on the porch swing creaked as they swung slowly back and forth.

"Father and I argued. We had a huge fight. He wanted me to wait another year to start taking classes. Said he needed me at the cafe. And he was probably right that he did need me. I now realize the stress he must have been under. But I wouldn't listen to him. I enrolled in that stupid writing class and took off for New Orleans one evening for the first class. I was so thrilled to be back in school. The atmosphere of excitement of the beginning of the school year. A room of students eager to learn." Keely paused and the only sound was the creaking of the swing again.

"I got back from New Orleans late that night. I had gone out for coffee after class with some new people I had met. I remember singing at the top of my lungs on the drive home. I felt so free, so alive, for the first time in over a year." Keely's voice dropped lower, and she turned to look at him, pain etched across her face. "When I got home that night, Father was gone. He'd died of a heart attack. Of course they couldn't get a hold of me, I didn't have a cell phone back then."

"Mom fell apart. It was too much for her. I took over the cafe and scheduling all of Kat's appointments and that has been my life ever since. But I deserve it. If I had only listened to my father and waited another year. But, no. I was selfish. I wanted those two nights a week all to myself. My escape."

"You can't blame yourself for your father's death. One argument doesn't cause a person to die. You know he must have had heart disease, right?"

"I only know he asked me not to go. To wait another year. To stay and help him. But I didn't."

"It wasn't really your responsibility to save your father's business, or the family, or any of that. You were so young. Your parents were supposed to be... well, parents. They made choices. Your mother could have worked more, they could have hired more staff."

"Money was really tight then. We spent so much money for Kat's medical bills and converting the house so it was wheelchair friendly."

Hunt wrapped his arm around her and pulled her close. "I'm so sorry. I wish I would have been here. Found some way to help."

"It wasn't yours to fix. But you know who did help a lot? Kevin. I think he felt sorry for us. He actually built the ramp into the house and repaired I don't know how many things for me at the cafe. He was so handy at stuff like that. He always had some silly story to tell Katherine to make her laugh."

Hunt's stomach rolled, and he clenched his jaw. Kevin's secret wrapped around him like barbed wire, digging at him, taunting him if he tried to move or breathe.

"Anyway, I owe it to my father to keep the cafe going. Provide for Kat and Mother. Writing was just a crazy dream of mine." Keely stared out into the darkened yard.

Two secrets revealed in one night.

Hunt sat in silence, holding Keely against him. Any words he had to say that could help her were lodged firmly in his throat.

Keely had turned down Hunt's offer to walk her home. She walked home alone every night. She sure didn't need an escort tonight. The town was as safe as any town could be these days. Besides, her walk home from work gave her time to unwind from the day. Not to mention she was feeling uncomfortable about sharing all her guilt with Hunt. He probably didn't understand anyway. He'd always been free to do what he wanted. Travel. No responsibilities. He just couldn't understand what it was like to have no choice. And his remarks about how everyone had choices just grated on her. She didn't have a choice. Not at all.

She looked up at the moon, brightly lighting up the sky. It was either almost a full moon, or maybe just past a full moon. Waxing or waning so slightly she couldn't tell. When she was young, she'd always kept track of when the next full moon would be in her journal. She wondered when she'd stopped doing that. Probably after Kat's accident. It had seemed frivolous to look forward to such a silly thing as a full moon.

She reached her house after a few minutes' walk and turned for one last glance at the moon before heading in the house. The front room was empty, but she could see the kitchen lights spilling out into the hall. She walked back to see who was still up. Katherine sat in her wheelchair pulled up to the kitchen table with papers spread out before her.

"Hey there, KitKat, what are you up to?"

"You haven't called me KitKat in years." Katherine looked up from her papers and smiled. "I've kind of missed it."

Keely dropped down into the chair beside her sister. "Summerfest plans?"

"I'm just making some notes to talk to Bella about tomorrow. We're going to meet at the cafe before she opens the shop. Can I catch a ride with you in the morning?"

"I leave really early. I could come back and get you."

"No, that's okay. You don't have to make a second trip. I'll go in with you and keep working on my plans until Bella shows up."

Keely nodded. "Mom go up to bed already?"

"She did. After arguing with me about working on planning Summerfest. And watching Natalie's boys." Katherine grinned. "Oh, and let's not forget me learning the books at the cafe and the—*and I quote verbatim*—the silly, ridiculous patio that's just a waste of good money."

"Well, I see she at least has her list of complaints at the ready."

"And I think I found a car and a guy who can convert it to hand controls for me." Katherine pushed a paper over with precisely written notes and a total for the car and conversion. "Do you think we can swing this? Is it too much?"

"Not at all. Very reasonable." *Where the heck was she going to come up with the ready cash?*

"I'm sure it will take me a while to learn to drive again, especially using the hand controls. But I'd like to get my license again. I want the independence."

"Well, we'll make it work to buy the car then." Keely quickly tried to figure how to rob Peter to pay Paul. Or more likely rob the renovation fund to pay for the car. But she'd find a way to make it work. Katherine didn't ask for much.

"And after I meet with Bella, I thought we could start working on me learning the books?"

Keely made a mental note to adjust the renovation budget first thing in the morning, before they started into learning the books, so Katherine would have no idea where the car funds came from. "That sounds fine. We'll do it after the morning crowd." She got up from the table, suddenly very tired. "You need anything before I go up?"

"No, I'm fine. I'm just going to finish up a few notes, then I'll head for bed, too. I'll see you early in the morning."

"You sure you want to get up that early?"

"I'm sure. Night, Keely."

"Night KitKat."

CHAPTER 9

"Boys, come on. We're going to be late." Bella felt a stab of guilt at the two bowls of cereal sitting on the table. A better mother would be providing a hot breakfast for her children, but she'd lost track of time this morning. They would at least have orange juice with their cereal and she'd packed them both a healthy lunch. That was the best she could do today.

Timmy came wandering out of his room, school backpack dangling from one arm. "Mom, I can't find my shoes."

"Okay, sit down and eat and I'll look for them." Bella walked over by the couch and scooped up one lone tennis shoe. That wasn't going to help much. "Jeremy. You're going to go to school without breakfast if you don't hurry up."

Jeremy trudged into the kitchen, a scowl on his face. "I forgot to do a stupid worksheet last night."

"You told me you had your homework finished before you played your video game last night."

"Well, I forgot about it."

Bella wasn't convinced. Jeremy had gotten a new video game yesterday and had been anxious to play it.

"You know the rules, homework before video games. Tonight I'll go through your assignment book with you after you finish your homework to make sure it's all complete." She'd been trying to teach Jeremy it was his responsibility to do his homework and take the consequences if he didn't finish, but it looked like she needed to spot check again for a while.

Jeremy plopped down in a chair and set a crumpled worksheet next to his bowl of cereal. He took bites of the cereal and scribbled answers with his pencil. Timmy reached for the bottle of orange juice and knocked into Jeremy's bowl, spilling cereal and orange juice all over the worksheet.

"Hey, stupid, look what you did." Jeremy grabbed his paper with orange juice dripping from it.

"You're stupid." Timmy retorted.

"Don't call your brother names." She pinned them both with a mom look.

Timmy looked close to tears. "I didn't mean to."

"It's okay. It was an accident." Bella grabbed a towel and wiped the orange juice from the paper and the table. She turned to Jeremy. "If you had done your homework last night, like you were supposed to, the paper wouldn't have been on the breakfast table."

"If Timmy wasn't such a baby, he wouldn't be spilling stuff all the time."

"Jeremy. That's enough. Finish your homework and your breakfast." Bella glanced at her watch. "Five minutes and we're walking out the door."

"I won't have my worksheet finished."

"Well, you'll have to turn it in unfinished, then."

Bella looked by the back door for Timmy's other shoe. Nothing. "Timmy, why don't you wear your old black tennis shoes today. We'll look for your new ones tonight."

"But the black ones hurt my feet."

Bella sighed. Of course they did, that's why she'd bought him the new ones. He was growing so quickly these days she could barely keep him in shoes and pants that fit. She got down on her hands and knees and peered under the couch. *Success.* She held up the shoe like a prized award. "Slip these on. We need to leave."

Two arguments in the car and one episode of name calling and she had the boys dropped off at school, with shoes and one unfinished worksheet.

She walked into the cafe a few minutes later, glad to have a chance to sit down and sip a cup of coffee without any spills or arguments. Katherine was sitting at a table by the window and waved to her.

Becky Lee came up and gave her a quick hug. "Hey, Izzy. I'll get you some coffee. Katherine said you were coming to work on the Summerfest plans."

Bella hugged her friend. Becky Lee always had a smile and a cheerful word for everyone. She was actually that rare breed that Bella could not understand—the kind who loved the early hours of the day and was actually chipper in the morning.

She sat down across from Katherine. "How's the planning going?"

"I made up a list of other stores in town that I think we should contact. I'm going to make some calls this afternoon."

"I talked to Jenny, who talked to the band director at the school. He's all excited about having the band march in the parade. The high school cheerleaders are all set to march, too. I also found out that Steve Bergeron —you know him, don't you? A builder here in town. He's friends with my brother, Gil. Anyway, he had a truck, a sound system he can run to play music, and a flatbed that we can use for a float."

Becky Lee dropped off a cup of coffee and hurried to wait on a new table of customers. Bella took a sip of the hot coffee. "Man, I love whoever invented coffee."

Katherine laughed. "I'm kind of that way about tea."

Bella opened up her ever-present notebook and dug in her purse for a pen. She carefully turned to the section on Summerfest and looked at her list. "Oh, and Doc Benson and Holly—she's the new vet that just came to town. She dates Steve Bergeron."

"The Steve of the truck, flatbed, and sound system?" Katherine smiled.

"Very same one. Well, they are going to have a float with one of the rescue groups with a few of the pets they'll have for adoption."

In a case of dueling notebooks, Katherine looked down at her list. "Miss Judy said her dance class could walk in the parade, too. They'll wear their costumes from their last recital. The Adventurer Club is going to be in it, too. The boys are so excited."

"I pity the leader keeping all those little boys in line in the parade." Bella grinned.

Katherine checked off her list. "I've gotten a lot of donations for the ice cream social on that Saturday afternoon. We have permission to have it in the town park. I have three bands set to play music that afternoon and evening in the park in the gazebo."

"Wow, impressive. You've been busy."

"It's the most productive I've felt in years. I love planning all this. I think it's all coming together nicely."

Katherine's eyes shown with enthusiasm. Bella could see this project was good for her.

"You know. I've felt like I've been Poor Katherine for years. The sad girl who was in that accident. I'm tired of that. I don't want anyone's pity I want people to see me as... well, as just Katherine."

"If people don't think you're capable after all this hard work, they're nuts. You've done such a great job. And I thought I was the ultimate planner. I think you might have to steal my title." Bella realized she'd been one of those people who thought of Katherine as Poor Katherine. That was ending right now. She'd grown into a capable young woman. "Okay, Just Katherine, let's get back to planning."

Katherine threw back her head and laughed out loud, her eyes sparkling with mirth. Bella saw Becky Lee look across the cafe, grin, and nod her head slightly. Bella smiled back.

~

Keely pulled the door of the Magnolia Cafe closed behind her. The cool night air draped around her as she dug in her purse, fumbling to find her keys. She sighed and dredged the fathomless depths until she finally felt the keys. With a triumphant flourish, she locked the door and dropped the keys back into the purse.

There were still quite a few people walking along Main Street tonight. The cafe closed at nine on weeknights and she'd managed to walk out the door not fifteen minutes later. She turned from the door and stepped out onto the sidewalk. Time to relax and let the stress of the day slip away.

"Well, hello there, Keely."

She looked up at the impeccably dressed woman standing before her with her arm entwined with a man in business suit that fairly screamed 'I have money.'

"Camille." She and Hunt should never had talked about her. It was like they'd conjured Camille's spirit from Mobile and dropped it to torment her right onto Main Street in Comfort Crossing.

"I see you're still working at your family's *diner*."

Technically the Magnolia Cafe was *almost* a diner. But Camille said the word like it was some kind of greasy-spoon truck stop.

"I am. Just closed up and headed home."

"This is Delbert Hamilton from the Hamilton Hotels. You've heard of them, right?" Camille clung to stuffy old Del's arm and practically simpered at him. "Delbert, this is Keely. She's a *waitress* at the *diner*."

Keely wasn't even going to rise to the bait. Camille knew darn well that she ran the *cafe* now and had for years.

"Please to meet you, ma'am." Old Delbert sounded anything but pleased, but obviously nothing would overcome his southern gentleman manners.

"Nice to meet you too, Del." Keely hid her smile when he grimaced at the nickname.

"Delbert and I are in town to visit Mama. She's throwing a big party this weekend to introduce Delbert to her friends."

"How nice." Keely worked up about as much sincerity as Delbert had shown to her.

"And how is poor Katherine doing these days?" Camille didn't wait for an answer and turned to Delbert. "Poor thing was in a car accident. She's in a wheelchair now." She said the word wheelchair in a whispered voice like it was something to be ashamed of.

Keely grit her teeth and pasted on a fake smile. "She is doing fabulous. She's heading up the Summerfest celebration that Comfort Crossing is having this summer. A parade, ice cream social, baseball game against Bayou Corner. Three days of fun. You really should come back to town for it. It's going to be great." The last thing she wanted was to see Camille, but then, she couldn't help but brag a bit on Kat.

"Oh, that does sound *precious,* but I doubt we'll be able to make it. We're thinking of heading to Europe this summer."

How nice for you. Maybe you could leave tonight.

"Come along, Delbert. We don't want to keep

Mama waiting. We're having drinks and dessert at Sylvia's Place. She doesn't close early like your little diner does. We're just hoping she has a decent bottle of wine. So hard to find that here in this little town. I keep apologizing to Delbert for the town's shortcomings, but Mama just refuses to leave, so I do have to come back here once in a while." Camille clutched at the I'm-made-from-money suit and flashed a vacuous smile at Keely. "So nice to see you. Must run."

And yet some more insincere words were flung her direction. Special.

She watched the two of them head down Main Street, Camille in her high heeled shoes, wobbling just a bit when they had to cross over the cobblestone street. Keely had to keep herself from uncharitably wishing Camille would take a fall...

CHAPTER 10

"**O**wen." Bella launched herself into his welcoming arms. "You're back."

Owen laughed and held her close. "That's some welcome."

"I've missed you." She hugged him tight then tilted her head up to kiss him. He obliged with a nice long, deep kiss and a bit of a rumbly noise in his chest, like he was just as glad to see her as she was to see him.

"Come inside." She opened the door wide, and they walked into the carriage house. "I didn't expect you until tomorrow."

"Got things wrapped up and came back early."

Bella looked around the house in dismay. A pair of roller skates sat in the middle of the floor. The boys' homework was spread across the kitchen table. One lone shoe of Timmy's, of course, was perched precariously on the edge of a chair. Dishes were scattered across the counter.

"The place is a mess." She really didn't want him to know how out of control things got around here when she was busy. She knew Owen came from a home where nothing had ever been out of place.

"Nope. It looks like a home." Owen smiled at her.

"Let me at least clear you a space." She picked up the boys' jackets from the end of the couch, stacked the magazines that were tossed on the chair and put them in a neat pile on the coffee table.

"Mom. Jeremy won't let me have my hat." Timmy came racing into the room and collided with Owen. "Oh. I'm sorry. Hi, Owen." He stepped back and looked up at Owen, an anxious look on his face.

"Not a problem. I was in the way. How've you been, Timmy?" Owen smiled at her son.

Jeremy came running out of Timmy's room with no hat in sight. "I don't have your stupid hat."

"Jeremy."

"I don't have your *silly* hat."

"You hid it."

"Did not."

Bella sighed. "Jeremy, mind your manners and say hi to Owen."

"Hello, Mr. Campbell."

No amount of Owen telling Jeremy that he could call him Owen seemed to work.

"Hey, Jeremy."

Jeremy barely nodded in reply.

She turned to her sons. "Jeremy, you have two minutes to come walking out here with Timmy's hat in your hand. Timmy, clean your homework off the table and wash up for dinner." Her sons scattered.

"Sorry about that. It's always a bit hectic at dinner time."

"I should have called first."

"No, you don't have to call. You're welcome anytime. You know that." But if he was going to just start dropping by, she was going to have to up her game in the housekeeping department. She looked around at the mess and sighed. More likely, Owen was going to have to just get used to the chaos.

"Let me get the boys fed and we can go out and sit on the porch. I just made up a pitcher of sweet tea."

And by boys fed, she meant pull out the frozen fish sticks she put in the oven and drop a dollop of applesauce on their plates. It had been one of those days.

She settled the boys at the dinner table with Timmy's hat placed directly in front of him on the table. No hats at the table rule twisted only slightly. She and Owen went out to the porch with two icy glasses of tea.

She slipped gratefully down on a rocker, glad to be off her feet. Owen leaned against the porch railing.

"How was your trip? Still snowing in Denver?"

"It was. But I got out between storms. That's why I'm early. Wrapped things up before the next wave of storms came through. They are getting a lot of snow this spring."

"Did you finalize the deal?"

"Just about. My lawyers are working out a few kinks, then the contract will be ready to sign. If all goes well, the Stanton hotel will be one of ours within a year's time."

Bella was amazed at how well Owen could negotiate deals. His line of boutique hotels was growing quickly. His company also owned various other companies related to the hotel industry, as well as a line of fancy restaurants, most of them in the hotels he owned. But still he came back to Comfort Crossing as often as possible.

"What are you thinking about?" Owen stretched out one long leg and adjusted his position on the railing.

"How lucky I am that you keep coming back to Comfort Crossing. I know you're really busy with work."

"I can do a lot of work anywhere as long as I have internet. I just wish I could spend more time here with you."

She wished he could, too. It seemed like just as soon as she got used to him being around, he was off again, whisking away to some far city or back to Chicago where his company was located.

"How are plans for Summerfest coming along?" Owen asked.

"Really well. Katherine is a great person to work with. She has so many good ideas. We have a lot of sponsors set up and events planned. I'm hoping it brings a lot of tourists to town. We've expanded it from just Saturday and Sunday to Thursday night through Sunday. The parade is on Saturday late morning. It just keeps getting bigger all the time."

"Sounds like you've been busy with all that. Things going okay at the shop?"

"It's a bit of a slow period before the summer tourist season. The weekends are picking up now that the weather is nicer. I think people come to town for a quick weekend outing. I'm still turning a profit and putting away some each month in hopes of buying the building from you."

"I told you that you don't have to do that. I'm not planning on renting it to anyone else."

"I appreciate all you did to find me this new place for the shop—you know that—but eventually I'd like to own the building and the carriage house."

"Whatever you want. I'm just glad it all worked out."

A crash came from inside the house. Bella rolled her eyes and slowly got to her feet. "I'll be right back. Let me see what mischief the boys are up to."

Owen watched Bella cross the porch and go back inside. He could hear the raised voices of the boys and Bella's calming voice drift out the screen door. He didn't know how she did it all. Raise the boys, run the shop, and now work on Summerfest. He was in awe of her. All he had to do was run his company and take care of himself. And he had people to help him with both of those.

He turned when he heard a car, the wheels crunching on the short gravel drive. Jenny and Clay stepped out of the car and waved. "Owen, I didn't know you were back in town." Jenny climbed the stairs and gave him a quick hug.

"Just got back." Owen reached over and shook Clay's offered hand. "Bella is inside. Some kind of commotion with the boys."

Jenny laughed. "Those two are a handful. I thought having just one that age was about all I could handle. It's supposed to get easier as they get older, and I guess things are easier with Nathan now that he can drive himself places, but it's always something, I guess. He's in the throes of being jilted by this girl he had a crush on. Very angsty time at our house."

"If you're looking for drama, you should try raising two girls." Clay shook his head. "It's one crisis after the next. Danielle's are usually based around boys or clothes. Abigail's are always about school. She is so hard on herself with schooling and she's only in grade school. I dread her teenage years."

Owen had no idea how people raised kids and stayed sane. It was all so foreign to him. His parents hadn't even really raised him. His nannies and private schooling had been the ones raising him.

"I'm going to run inside and see Izzy." Jenny went into the house.

Clay took a chair across from Owen and leaned back. "Jenny found something or other that she wanted to show Bella regarding the wedding."

"How are the wedding plans coming along?"

"I'm not sure. You have any idea the difference between pistachio, mint, or seafoam—they all look like green to me? Evidently choosing between one of those is a big decision."

"Not a clue. Whatever happened to good old plain green, like the crayon."

"I think if a color doesn't have a fancy name, it doesn't count in a wedding." Clay grinned. "Not that I'd deny Jenny anything. Whatever she wants to do regarding the wedding I agree to. I'm just so darn glad she's marrying me."

"They seem to be having a good time planning the wedding. Bella seems to be happiest when she's organizing something."

"I know she's been a big help to Jenns. I hope they're enjoying the planning. Me? I would have been just as happy to elope. Or just take the kids somewhere and have a quick ceremony. But Jenny wants a big wedding, so that's what she'll get."

Jenny and Bella came back outside with a pitcher of tea and more glasses. Bella filled tea glasses for everyone and sank back onto the rocker.

"Everything okay in there?"

"Just another hat scuffle. I swear Jeremy goes out of his way to push Timmy's buttons. I sent them both to their rooms to finish their homework."

"That Timmy is getting cuter by the day. I don't know how you can resist his impish smile." Jenny laughed. "I'd be letting him get away with murder."

"He is quite the sweetie, isn't he? But man, oh man, do they bicker a lot. But the funny thing is, they are also each other's biggest supporter. Some older kids were picking on Timmy the other day and Jeremy came to his rescue and sent them running off." Bella took a sip of her tea. "They do exhaust me, though."

Bella did look tired. She often looked worn out and Owen wished she'd let him get her some help. A cleaning lady, more help for the store, anything. But if he'd learned anything about Bella it was that she wanted to make it on her own. He admired her for it. Besides, even when she looked exhausted she seemed happy, like she wouldn't change a thing about her life.

"So, did you two get more wedding decisions made?"

"Yes, we've decided on mint green for the wedding."

Both women smiled delightedly so he figured that was a big decision to have made. What the heck did he know about weddings? He went to a few a year, mostly social commitments, nothing more. He only knew about them from the invited-out-of-obligation side. Bella, Jenny, and Becky Lee seemed to be having such fun organizing the wedding down to the littlest detail.

Jenny stood up. "Well, we should be going. I know you still need to check the boys' homework and get them to bed."

Clay stood up and Jenny walked over to him. He wrapped his arm around her shoulder as effortlessly as if drawing a breath. Owen envied that effortlessness. He still felt awkward with Bella at times. He wasn't used to having a serious relationship, and then as soon as he started to get used to it, he got called out of town.

"We'll see you two soon. Let's all try to get together for dinner. I'll call Becky Lee and see if we can get something set up." Jenny smiled up at Clay and they turned and headed to the car.

Bella sighed. "I'm just so happy for them. I can't wait until the wedding."

~

"You're deep in thought." Clay rested his hand on hers as they drove home from Izzy's.

"You're going to think I'm crazy." Jenny wasn't sure how to explain it to Clay.

"Try me."

"I just feel like something is… wrong. I've been feeling it ever since we started really planning this wedding and picked the date. I sometimes feel like it's not really going to happen."

"I've waited years and years for this wedding. I'm not going to let anything stop me now."

A shiver ran up Jenny's spine and she tried to talk herself out of her doubts. "I just have this weird feeling about the wedding."

"I'll marry you tomorrow at the Justice of the Peace if that will put your mind at ease. We could still have the wedding in June."

"And that is why I love you Clay Miller. Because you'd do just about anything for me, wouldn't you?" Jenny squeezed his hand. "I'm probably just being silly. It's probably just wedding jitters after waiting for so many years. I sometimes want to pinch myself to make sure I'm awake and this is really happening."

"It's happening, all right. I'm counting the days. The girls are getting excited about moving into our new house, too."

"Nathan is too, though I think he's a bit sad to be leaving the house he grew up in and all the memories there with his dad." Jenny's heart pounded when she realized what she'd said. "I'm sorry. That was thoughtless. I mean with Joseph."

"It's okay, Jenns. I know Joseph was a great dad to Nathan. Nothing will change that. Not even finding out I'm his biological father. It's all going to take time. I don't care that he thinks of Joey as his dad, I just hope he starts to think of me as his dad, too."

"I think he already does. You two seem to be getting closer. Just yesterday he was saying he wanted to talk to you about which science courses to take next year. Honestly, he's always been interested in law, like his grandfather. I mean Joseph's dad." There, she'd done it again. It was hard to retrain her thinking. She sighed. "Anyway, now a days he talks about possibly looking into premed when he goes away to college."

"Really?" Clay flashed a huge grin like a kid who'd been told he was getting just what he wanted for Christmas.

Jenny laughed. "Not to say he won't change his mind. But I think he does need to take an extra science class or two next year to see if that interests him. He's already talked to his advisor about moving some classes around."

"I'll talk to him tomorrow. You two are still planning on dinner at Mom's, right?"

"Yes, we'll be there. I hate that Greta is going to all that work."

"Oh, she loves to cook big meals and have family around. She does consider you family, you know."

"She's always been like a mom to me." Jenny thought back on the years in high school when she was dating Clay. They'd hung out at Greta's house all the time. Greta had always been so welcoming and accepting of her. So different than at her house. Her father had not liked Clay one bit and had gone so far as to tell Clay that he'd disown Jenny if Clay kept seeing her. The beginning of the end for them. Until, miraculously, they'd found each other again seventeen years later and it had all worked out. Not that her father was pleased now, either. But she was a grown woman now, and really didn't care what a judgmental, grouchy old man thought. Her mother was pleased though, and that meant a lot to Jenny.

Her thoughts circled back to the wedding and the vague sense of unease. She shook her head. *Wedding jitters. That must be all it was.*

CHAPTER 11

Hunt was going to ask her.

No, he wasn't.

Yes. Yes, he was. If he could just get up the nerve. What was the worst thing that could happen? Keely said no?

She won't say no, will she?

"Earth to Hunt. You're just standing there looking off into space. We need to get going or I'll be late to my shift at the cafe." Natalie poked his arm. "What are you thinking about?"

"Whether to ask Keely to go away with me for the weekend. I got a quick photography assignment down on the gulf coast. Documenting some small towns that rebuilt after that series of hurricanes came through." Hunt tilted his head to one side, then back again. "I think it would be good for her to get away. Katherine has learned so much about the business in the last month. If you and Becky Lee help her, I'm sure she could run the cafe for a few days, don't you think?"

"I'm sure Katherine could do it, and, of course, we'll help. I guess the big question is whether Keely will be able to let go of the control long enough to give her sister a chance. I know Katherine has told me she wants to do more."

"I think it's hard for Keely to look at Katherine with new eyes. To see the woman she's become. She seems very capable."

"She's a quick learner, that's for sure. She already knows so much about the business, though I'm sure some of it is from growing up with the cafe being owned by her parents. But she told me she's taken over payroll from Keely. She's been learning inventory, too. She is so excited when she talks about the running of the cafe. I think she has a real knack for it."

"Well, I'm hoping Keely will give her a chance to run it for a few days."

"Hoping she'll go away with you, you mean." Natalie grinned at him.

"That, too." He felt a wave of heat wash over his face.

"Hunt Robichaux. I do believe you have a crush on her. I knew you'd been going out a few times, but look at you. I can't remember the last time I've seen you interested in someone."

"We're just friends." That sounded weak, even to him. "I mean, I like her… it's just… complicated."

"Isn't it always?" Natalie scooped up her purse. "Let's get to the cafe. No time like the present to ask her."

"I haven't actually decided if I'm going to ask her."

"Yes, you have. You're asking her." His sister turned her back on him to silence any more argument and headed out the door.

He followed her out to the truck and all the way to the cafe he mentally rehearsed asking Keely.

Keely looked up to see Hunt and Natalie walk in the door to the cafe. She hadn't seen Hunt since he took her to a movie two days ago. Her heart skipped a beat when he flashed a smile her direction. Though, that was silly. He was going to leave soon. There was really no point in getting worked up about his good looks, sexy smile, or the way he sort of took her breath away when he kissed her. No. No reason to think about that at all.

Natalie walked over and tucked her purse under the counter. "Hunt has something he wants to ask you."

Hunt shot his sister a nasty glance.

What was that all about?

Before Hunt had a chance to say anything, Kat came rolling out of the office. "Hi, you two."

"Hi, Katherine. I was just saying that Hunt has something to ask Keely." Natalie shot back a pointed look at her brother.

Katherine looked at Hunt expectantly. Hunt glared at his sister. "What Natalie is so *kindly* butting in about is… well, I wondered if you'd like to go down to the gulf coast with me for a few days. I have a photo assignment

I picked up. Thought you might like to tag along. Take a few days off."

"Oh, I don't know…" She couldn't just up and leave the cafe for days.

"Sounds like a great idea to me. When are you leaving?" Katherine jumped in.

"I have to leave within a few days to get there and take the photos and get them sent in by my deadline."

"Perfect. Leave tomorrow. I'll be fine here with the cafe." Katherine nodded her head.

"I'll pick up some extra shifts while you're gone. Jenny found me a great high school girl for a sitter for evenings and weekends now that Katherine is working so much at the cafe. I'll call her to watch the boys." Natalie added her agreement.

"I can't just leave." Keely felt a mild panic rise up in her. She had to be here, it was her responsibility.

Becky Lee walked up to the counter and set down a pitcher of tea. "What's up?"

"We're just convincing Keely to go away to the coast for a few days with Hunt. Take a quick vacation," Katherine said.

"Sounds like a fabulous idea." Becky Lee agreed with Katherine. "I can work extra if you need me."

"It's all settled then. You leave tomorrow." Katherine said it like it was all decided.

But it wasn't. She couldn't just leave the place to run itself.

"I've got this. Really. You go and have a good time. When is the last time you've gotten away? Heck, when

have you even taken a day off? It will be good for you."
Katherine looked at her expectantly.

"I don't know." Keely felt herself wavering. Kat had
learned a lot in the last month or so, and if Natalie and
Becky Lee were around, too… How long had it been
since she'd taken a break? She couldn't even remember
the last time.

"So, what do you say?" Hunt looked at her with that
darn irresistible smile.

"Okay, okay. You think we could be back in
two days?"

"Three or four days would work, too." Katherine
grinned. "How much could go wrong here in just a
handful of days?"

Keely gave up. There was no way she could argue
with all of them. Besides, the idea was starting to have a
bit of an appeal.

"I'll pick you up at eight tomorrow morning."

"Pick me up here at the cafe. I'll get it
opened and—."

"Keely means to pick her up at home. I'll open the
cafe tomorrow," Katherine interrupted.

"I've got the morning shift tomorrow. We'll be fine.
Honest. Go have fun." Becky Lee grabbed some menus
and went to greet a group of customers who had just
walked in.

"Katherine, let's go check the schedule and see when
else Becky Lee and I can help." Natalie headed back
towards the office and Katherine followed behind her,
stopping at a table to chat briefly with Widow Schneider.

"I guess it's all settled then?" Hunt raised one eyebrow.

"I guess it is." Keely wasn't sure how she'd been talked into this. Her mind immediately went into overdrive. She'd sit down and make a list of things that Kat needed to remember to do. Kat could always call if she had questions, right?

"I'll see you in the morning, then."

Keely nodded and watched him walk to the door. He paused briefly and turned to her, flashing that disarming smile of his. No fair that he had such a secret weapon at his disposable. She would see him in the morning… unless she talked herself out of it.

CHAPTER 12

Hunt was up early the next morning, helping Natalie get the boys ready for school. He'd promised her he'd run the boys to school on his way to pick up Keely. Everything was going smoothly, except for missing homework, and they were out of bread to make sandwiches for lunch—he'd forgotten he told Natalie he'd go shopping. Natalie found some tortillas in the fridge and saved the day by convincing the boys that the new trendy thing in school lunches was wraps.

"Boys, go upstairs and finish getting ready. You're leaving in ten minutes." Natalie stood in the kitchen, packing up three lunch sacks.

"I told you Nat, I'm a dangerous one to give any responsibility." Hunt shook his head. She'd given him one thing to do yesterday. Grocery shop. Failure. Big failure. "I'm sorry."

"It's not a big deal. I know you've been really busy with the patio, and now this photography assignment.

Besides, it's not your responsibility to do these things, it's mine."

"I'm trying to help, though. I've just never been any good at being the one for people to depend on."

"You talking about forgetting to go to the market, or are you talking about Mama?"

Hunt swallowed. "Maybe a bit of both. Trying to make things up to you."

"She wasn't your fault. It wasn't even your responsibility to save her."

But he'd *felt* like it was his duty to save her and protect Natalie. "I tried though. And I tried to keep you with me after she died, but Dad was so angry at me. He sent you off to live with Aunt Mae your senior year of high school."

"It was probably for the best. Gave you a chance to chase your dream of photography, instead of being saddled with a little sister here in Comfort Crossing." Natalie walked over and rested her hand on his arm. "You know, it was Mama's fault, not yours. No one can make a person stop drinking if they don't want to. Not even you."

Hunt stared down at his sister's hand. "I just wanted to make things right for you, give you some kind of home life."

"I know you were always protecting me from the fallout of her drinking. Dad just went out of town all the time so he could ignore it. I think Mama drank because she was so miserable. Miserable being married to Dad. Miserable having hardly any money. I'm pretty sure being a mom wasn't her thing either. She was a sad, lonely woman. I'm not sure how you could have fixed any of that."

"But, when I came home that night and found her... I just felt like I should have been able to do something more. Stop her. Get her help."

"She drank, Hunt. Her choice. That night she drank way too much and fell and hit her head."

"If I would have come home earlier, instead of hanging out with Kevin, then maybe..."

"Hunt, you couldn't have changed a thing."

"But I so wanted to be here for you, give you some kind of home life for your last year in high school, keep you from having to move to Hattiesburg to Aunt Mae's and change schools."

"It was one year. One year. I was so upset when it happened. Who wants to change schools their senior year of high school? But it all worked out okay. Kevin started coming to see me most weekends. So, maybe you should look at it as you gave Kevin and me the opportunity to be together."

"Maybe." But Hunt didn't believe her. Anytime he took on a responsibility, it seemed like he failed. "I've failed at more than that with horrible consequences."

"What are you talking about?"

"This young kid. A photojournalist. He was with me on one of my assignments. Terrible place to be. Warring factions." Hunt clenched his teeth, then took a deep breath. "He begged me let him tag along with me one day. I shouldn't have. But once I said yes, it was my responsibility to get him back to safety. I knew the ropes. I knew the danger."

Hunt's stomach clenched like it always did when he thought about the young man. A boy really. Twenty-two years old and living in darkness now.

"I couldn't keep him safe. He's blind now. A blind photographer."

"I'm so sorry. I didn't know." Natalie walked up and placed her hand on his arm. "But you know what? Somehow you're going to have to find a way to forgive yourself. Realize it's not all your fault, and the young man chose to go with you. All we can do is try our best, Hunt. That's all any of us can do."

Hunt nodded and turned away from Natalie, not truly believing her, because he still felt like he'd failed his mom. He'd failed his sister. And he sure as heck had failed that young photojournalist.

Which was why his motto now was to avoid responsibilities. Not have people depend on him. So far, it seemed to be working just fine. Except for the fact that Natalie was starting to depend on him some, and he'd taken on fixing up the patio for Keely and had promised it finished by Summerfest... and neither were really working out very well.

To Keely's utmost surprise, she didn't talk herself out of leaving. She'd made up a massive to-do-remember-this-don't-forget list for Kat and made her promise to call if she had any questions. Any at all. Katherine had just laughed at her and shooed her out the door.

So here she was, riding down the coast highway with

Hunt, windows down in the truck. The truck Hunt had sworn Natalie wouldn't need while they were gone. Becky Lee had promised to give Natalie a ride if needed, but Natalie had said she'd probably just walk. It wasn't more than fifteen minutes from her house to the Magnolia Cafe. Still, Keely couldn't quiet the list of things that might go wrong that was swirling around in her mind.

She shook her head, determined to forget the cafe—as if that were even possible—and turned to Hunt. "So, tell me about your assignment."

"It's for a regional magazine. They want a series of photos of the small towns along the coastline of Mississippi, Alabama, and the Florida panhandle, showing how they've recovered from the series of hurricanes that have hit this area in the last years. New Orleans has gotten a lot of coverage since Katrina, but this is more focused on some of the smaller towns." Hunt nodded to a map on the seat between them. "I've plotted out some towns I want to visit. I thought we'd just drive and make our way down the coast."

"Sounds like a plan." Well, actually it didn't sound like a plan. It sounded like a non-plan. No specifics of where and when. No reservations on where to stay. Just wandering. And that, in and of itself, sounded wonderful to her.

She leaned back on the seat and watched the coast out the window. The road swerved close to the sea at points, then wound its way back inland again. A cool breeze blew in the open windows, making a riotous mess of her hair. She dug in her purse for a clip and fastened her hair back. Loose locks still tickled her face as they managed to escape.

"You enjoying yourself?" Hunt's deep voice interrupted her thoughts.

"I am. Surprisingly so. It's been so long since I've gotten away. I can't even remember the last time. Truly, I think it was before the accident."

"That's a long time to never take a break. It's sometimes good to do things just for yourself."

"Well, I've been so busy. I didn't think I could get away. There was no one to run the cafe, and it's what supports us." A pretty good list of excuses if she did say so herself.

"I'm glad you decided to let Kat have a go at running it for a few days. She looked kind of excited to have the opportunity."

"She did, didn't she? I hope everything works out okay. I told her to call if she had any problems."

"I bet you don't get that call. She seemed determined to make it work on her own. Besides, what could go wrong in just a few days?"

Natalie was determined to help Kat in any way possible. She wanted to make sure things went smoothly while Keely was away. It was the least she could do. She owed their family that much. Keely would get a much needed break and Katherine would prove to herself she was capable of running the cafe.

The first morning, right after Keely left town, the

dishwasher person quit, and they got backed up on running the dishes. Not a problem. Natalie was just going to stay after her shift and get them caught up.

Melanie came hurrying out of the kitchen towards the end of the breakfast rush. "We don't have any water."

Katherine's eyes widen. "No water at all? Now what do we do?"

"Let me call the water company." Natalie grabbed her phone from her pocket.

"Let me just look down the street." Becky Lee popped her head out the door. "Don't bother to call. The water company is out here on Main. There's water pouring down the street. Must be a break somewhere. I'll run and check and see when they think the water will be turned back on." Becky Lee hurried outside.

"I have two more tables to cook for. Glad it happened at the end of the breakfast crowd." Melanie looked around the cafe. "I can finish up cooking those meals, but we'll need to shut down after that until the water comes back on. Gotta get the breakfast dishes all cleaned—we're all behind on that. What a day to get behind on washing dishes. Plus, I know we need a working restroom, by health code."

Natalie hadn't even thought of the legal ramifications. Anyway, it didn't matter, because they'd close until the water came back on.

Becky Lee came rushing back in, slightly winded from hurrying down the street and back. "Looks like it won't be back until this afternoon sometime."

"We'll close for lunch and see if we can get things

cleaned up and open for dinner." Katherine sighed. "Some job I'm doing of running the cafe."

"Katherine, even Keely couldn't control this. Don't worry. We'll get back up and open soon." Natalie put her hand on Katherine's shoulder and squeezed it. Katherine looked devastated. "It's going to be okay. Don't worry."

Just then Katherine's mother came through the door. "What's going on? I saw the water trucks down on Main Street. We don't have any water at the house."

"We don't have water here, either, Mother. I'm going to close down for lunch and we'll try to open back up by dinner."

"I knew Keely shouldn't have left town. Just look at this mess." Mrs. Granger stood with her hands on her hips.

"I doubt if Keely could have prevented this either." Natalie tried to soften Mrs. Granger's harsh words.

Mrs. Granger turned to face Natalie, eyes flashing. "Keely had no business leaving Katherine alone to run this restaurant. She doesn't need the stress. It isn't good for her."

"Mother, it's okay. We'll just close down until the water is back on. Get things cleaned up, and then hopefully be ready for by dinner."

"You should go home and rest. You can't work all day and all night. You need a break."

"Keely works all day and all evening. Every single day. Day in and day out. I think it's about time we help her out and let her have a break." Katherine looked at her mother.

"It's just too much for you, Katherine dear."

"No, Mother, it's not. I'm fine. Why don't you go to the market and pick up some bottled water for the house? At least you'll have that."

"You come home for lunch, then. Take a break." Mrs. Granger seemed to back down a bit.

"I'll try, Mother." Katherine's tone of voice sounded more placating than convincing.

"And call Keely and get her back here to fix this." Mrs. Granger took one more look at Katherine and flounced out the door. That was the only word Natalie could think of to describe how the woman walked away.

"Don't even think about calling Keely," Katherine warned.

Natalie nodded in agreement.

Becky Lee delivered the food to the last two tables and told the customers they'd be shutting down as soon as they finished eating. Katherine gave the last few tables their meals for free. As the last customers walked out, Natalie put the closed sign up on the door.

Melanie came out of the kitchen. "I still have this pot of coffee. Anyone want to have a cup? Won't be any good by dinner time."

"I do." Katherine wheeled over to a clean table.

"Count me in. Then I'll clean up these last tables." Becky Lee perched on a chair beside Katherine.

"Coffee sounds great." Natalie grabbed some coffee cups and joined the women.

They sat and sipped their coffee and speculated about how long it would take until the water came back on. Natalie just hoped it would be back on in time for the dinner crowd, because she knew that missing lunch and dinner business would strain the already tight finances of the cafe. Keely had made no secret that things were tough with the cafe these days. That was part of why she wanted to add the patio, get the liquor license, and try to get more customers into the cafe. The profit from each day helped with that goal. But a day without any lunch or dinner would surely tank any profits from this week. The fresh pies wouldn't be so fresh tomorrow. The meatloaf special was already made and in the fridge, waiting to be cooked for dinner. If they couldn't open for dinner, they'd just have to find a way to save all the things Melanie had already gotten ready for the day.

Katherine set down her coffee cup. "So, are we all in agreement that no one calls Keely, and if she calls, no one mentions this?"

Natalie, Becky Lee, and Melanie nodded.

CHAPTER 13

Hunt pulled into the parking lot of a small motel along the coast of Mississippi. "Let's try this one. It had good reviews online."

Keely looked at him in surprise.

He laughed. "Yes, I did a bit of advance planning and looked up some possible places to stay. It doesn't matter much to me where I stay, but I didn't want to take you to some dumpy place. The reviews for this one says it's quaint and clean. Thought that would appeal to you."

"Well, you're right. That does appeal to me. I just thought you always did spontaneous stops."

"Well, then. I guess I'm just full of surprises."

They headed into the motel and rang the bell on the counter. An older man with a weathered face and a slope to his shoulders came out of the back room.

"Good evening. Looking for a room?"

"Two rooms, please. For one night." Hunt saw the desk clerk raise one eyebrow, but nod.

"Two rooms it is. Just passing through?"

"I'm actually doing a photo assignment. Small towns after the recent hurricanes the last few years."

"We sure got hit by a doozie with the hurricane a few years ago. I'm just getting the place opened back up. Fought with the insurance company but ended up dumping my life savings back into re-opening the place. My name is Frank, by the way." The owner held out his hand.

Hunt shook the man's hand. A firm handshake.

"Would you mind if I took a few photos of the place? Do you have any photos of the damage?"

"Wouldn't mind a bit. The town could use a touch of publicity to show how far we've come with rebuilding the area."

Hunt had the man sit behind the counter with some photos of the damage in his hands. The evening light streamed through a side window, perfect lighting for the photograph. He glanced over and saw Keely was writing in a small notebook she'd taken from her purse. He'd have to ask her about that. That was the third time today she'd written in the notebook. They chatted a bit longer with Frank and he recommended a diner in town for dinner. He swore they had the best shrimp on the coast.

Frank gave them the keys to their rooms. "Let me know if I can get you anything."

"Thanks, Frank. I'll be sure and let you know when the article comes out."

Hunt led the way to find their rooms. They were side by side near the back of the motel, away from the road noise. Keely said she'd be ready in thirty minutes for dinner. Hunt was pretty sure that was code for she was going to call Katherine and see how things were going at the cafe.

Hunt looked at his watched. He was dying to look at the photos he'd taken today. He'd just enough time to off load some of the photos from the memory card. He dumped the photos from his camera onto his laptop, quickly going through each one and flagging the photos he wanted to take a closer look at tonight. He typically worked late into the night when he was on assignment, sorting through the photos, and trying to come up with the ones he wanted to send in. He was pretty sure he'd process this whole series in black and white. It seemed to fit the mood of the series.

A knock at the door made him look up from his work and glance at his watch. He went to open the door.

"You ready?" Keely stood there looking at him expectantly. She had a just scrubbed look about her, with no hint they'd just spent a day in the truck driving and stopping at small towns along the way. She looked good. *Really good.*

"Um, yep. Just a sec." He shut his laptop and grabbed his camera, just in case.

They walked down the street to the diner. Frank had assured them it was only a short stroll away. The diner sat overlooking the coastline. As they entered the restaurant they were surrounded by the smell of fried fish, the clatter of dishes, and laughter coming from a group of people sitting near the back.

"Just take a seat anywhere." A waitress motioned to them.

They found a table near the window and the waitress dropped off menus for them. "Be back in flash. Just gotta give that table over there their check."

He watched in fascination as Keely took in every little detail of the diner. The old formica tabletops with a boomerang pattern on them. Vinyl booths. Cheery lighting. A long soda counter across one side of the diner with bright red stools. Almost every stool was in use. A table of kids looking about high school age sat near the back, drinking shakes and sharing a huge plate of french fries. Only two waitresses bustled around serving everyone, but they seemed to be keeping up with the dinner crowd.

"Scouting out the competition?"

Keely turned to him and smiled. "Can't help it. It's so interesting to see another small restaurant and how they are run. The place is doing a great business, but those two waitresses are keeping up with it all. And it's so light in here. No dim corners. That one back corner at Magnolia Cafe has always been dark. I think I'll look into new lighting for it when we get back."

The waitress came, and they ordered a plate of fried shrimp, a plate of garlic buttered shrimp, and a side of fried onion rings to share.

"Enough analyzing of the diner. How did your photos turn out? I noticed you were looking at them when I came and got you for dinner."

"I got some really good ones. That old abandoned school up the coast? Got some good ones of that. And the church that had reopened but still had the pile of boards and bricks outside? That one turned out well, too. I also liked the one with the old live oak surviving next to the cement foundation that was all that was left of that one house on the point."

"So all you saw was the destruction?" Keely's eyes bore into him.

He shifted uneasily on the vinyl seat. "What do you mean?"

"Didn't you see the spirit of the people? The old lady at the church who was so proud they'd fixed the church up enough for the Ladies' Prayer Meeting. The mobile homes sitting on oceanside lots while the owners rebuilt their original houses. The grouping of trailers on the school lot used as classrooms? These are people who love their towns and are sticking with them, no matter what Mother Nature dishes out."

Hunt hadn't looked at it in that way at all. He'd focused on the destruction, not the rebirth. All of a sudden he thought his focus of his photo series was wrong. Terribly wrong.

Keely looked at Hunt. He had an almost guilty look spreading across his face. Now she felt badly, but it was like they'd been in two different places today.

"I guess I just hadn't looked at it from your point of view." Hunt's face was creased in thought. "I'm not sure that your perspective isn't a better one than I was going with."

"Maybe you could do it from both perspectives. The destruction and the rebirth. Side by side."

Hunt stared at her then scrubbed his hands over his face. "That's a darn fine idea."

Keely laughed. "Don't look so surprised."

"Sorry. I just hadn't thought of it from any way but the destruction and ruin. Your idea is a better theme for the shoot." He looked at her. "So, what were you writing in your notebook all day? Do you mind if I ask?"

"I was writing down my thoughts on what we were seeing. Some remarks the people made. I don't know, it was like I was back to my journalism days in high school. I couldn't help myself."

Hunt stroked his chin. "So, what if you write the article up and I'll submit it along with my photos? There is no guarantee they'd take the article, but it's worth a shot. I could put in a good word with my editor."

"Really?" Keely's mind was reeling with possibilities of angles for the article. "I would love that. If nothing else it will be really great to write again."

"It's settled. We'll go from the rebirth angle versus the destruction angle. How about you come back to the room and help me pick out some photos?"

"I'd like that. Then I'll start writing."

Hunt grinned. "It's almost like old times, isn't it? The dynamic duo back in action."

It did feel like old times. Working together, grabbing a bite to eat, looking at his photos. Only now the photos were on his computer instead of hanging up in his darkroom.

The waitress delivered their meal, and Keely attacked it with relish. She was famished, whether from the fresh air and walking around today, or from the unexpected thrill of writing again, she wasn't sure. She even squabbled with Hunt over the last onion ring until he graciously decided they'd split it.

Keely watched Hunt as he stared out the window of the diner, lost in thought, his strong jawline etched against fading sunset. He raked his fingers through his hair and crooked one corner of his mouth. She remembered that look so well. It was his I'm-thinking look. He turned from the window and reached across the table and took her hand.

"This is great. I'm going to enjoy working with you again. My photo assignments, well I've enjoyed them, but it gets lonely out there by myself all the time."

"But you get to travel all over and go where you want. Choose the assignments that interest you. That sounds like a fantasy life to me."

"A lonely fantasy life. It's what I do, and I do enjoy the freedom, don't get me wrong. My only responsibility is to get my assignments in on time. I can handle that one duty. I do like that. But after these months back in Comfort Crossing with Natalie and the boys, well, I can see why it appeals to her to live in one place and just enjoy her kids."

"Living in one town my whole life seems so stifling. There is so much to see and explore." Keely sighed. "But, that doesn't really matter. I have the life I have."

"Maybe Katherine can help out more, and you could take some time off to travel."

"I don't know. We'll have to see how it goes with her taking over these few days. I talked to her tonight, and she sounded harried, but said everything was doing just fine. I'm not sure that I believed her."

Becky Lee gave a new order to Melanie and glanced back at the crowded cafe. The water had come back on at five tonight and the cafe had been full of people ever since. They'd rushed to keep up with the backlog of dishes and the throng of people. It seemed like everyone in Comfort Crossing had decided to go out to eat tonight after a significant portion of the town had been without water all day. It looked like they'd for sure make up for missing out on the lunch crowd. Too bad the patio wasn't up and running yet. The benches outside the cafe were crowded with people waiting for a table.

"Table three is asking for their check." Natalie nodded back towards the corner.

"Okay, thanks. You doing okay?"

"It's the busiest it's been since I've worked here, but I'm keeping up. I think." Natalie hurried away to place another order.

Slowly they made their way through the backup of customers. There was finally no waiting list and the last customers were finishing up. Becky Lee groaned a bit when she heard the front door open again. They were never going to get out of here tonight. She pasted on what she hoped looked like a sincere smile and turned to greet the customers.

Camille. Just what she needed.

"Hello, Camille. We're just closing up."

"So early?" Camille fluttered her hand on the arm of the man she was with.

"We usually close at nine, but we kept the cafe open late tonight since the water was out for most of the day for the town. Lots of folks just wanted to eat out."

"In Mobile we usually don't even consider going out to dinner until eight-thirty or so at the earliest."

How nice for you. But Becky Lee kept her thoughts to herself. "Melanie has already started closing down the kitchen. It's been a long day. I can offer you some pie and coffee if you like."

"What do you think, Delbert? You know, I think we should just go down to Sylvia's Place. She stays open until a respectable time."

The quiet little Delbert nodded his head.

"Oh, where are my manners?" Camille preened a bit. "This is Delbert Hamilton. Of the Hamilton hotels. You've heard of them? Delbert, honey, this is Becky Lee."

"Hey, Delbert, nice to meet you." Old Delbert looked like he wasn't sure she should be on a first name basis with him.

Delbert nodded his head again.

"Well, so *nice* to see you, Becky Lee," Camille said without a trace of sincerity.

So nice to see you leave. "Y'all have a nice evening." Becky Lee said it but didn't mean it. She couldn't care less if Camille and Old Delbert had a nice evening. The woman just got under her skin.

Becky Lee flipped the closed sign on the door, though, to be honest, everyone in Comfort Crossing knew they closed at nine during the week. Becky Lee did feel a twinge of guilt, a very minor twinge, that she was pretty sure Sylvia's Place was in the area of town that still didn't have their water back on. Oh well, Camille and good old Delbert might have to cook their own dinner tonight. Or more likely, get her mama's cook to make them something.

Katherine came up to her. "Was that Camille? Keely said she was in town."

"Yep. And some guy named Delbert Hamilton of the Hamilton hotels. I'm pretty sure Camille thinks that's his whole name."

Katherine grinned. "Looks like you were just about as pleased to run into her as Keely was."

"It's been kind of peaceful around these parts without Camille putting everyone in their place. I could never cotton to her attitude. Not sure why she thinks she is all that and a biscuit. Not very charitable on my part, though. Sent her on her way to Sylvia's Place."

"Isn't that area still without water?"

"I reckon so." Becky Lee grinned and turned back to her last customers who were just finishing up.

She finally closed and locked the door a little after ten. She cleared off her last table and headed to the kitchen, the tub of dishes balanced on her hip. Melanie was cleaning the grill, one hand perched against her arched back. "You okay, Melanie?"

"Just tired. My back is acting up a bit, but I'll be fine."

Katherine rolled into the kitchen. "Well, that was some night, wasn't it? I haven't seen the cafe that busy in years. Maybe we need more afternoons with no water."

"Bite your tongue. That was busy, though, wasn't it? Like the old days when there were only two places in town to eat." Becky Lee set the tub of dishes on the counter.

"We'd need more workers if that was how busy we were all the time," Katherine said.

"Workers who actually stayed and worked. Unlike the dishwasher kid who quit on us this morning." Melanie sat on a stool by the food prep counter.

Natalie came into the kitchen with a handful of glasses stacked up. "This is the last of the dishes from the counter."

"Natalie, why don't you go home. Go rescue the sitter. Melanie and Katherine, you go, too. I'll finish up the dishes." Becky Lee headed over to the dishwashing station. "Natalie, take my car and drive Katherine home. I'll just walk home when I'm finished."

"You sure?" Natalie set down the glasses.

"I'm sure. Go get some rest, and we'll hit it again tomorrow. Doubt if it will be as crazy as tonight."

"Thanks." Katherine looked exhausted.

Becky Lee was fairly certain Mrs. Granger would be sure to comment on Katherine's tired look as soon as she got home. The woman never missed a chance to nag her daughters. Ah, another uncharitable thought. She blamed it on the fact she herself was exhausted.

"Keely called me tonight, but I didn't say anything. Just said things were fine," Kat admitted.

"I'm thinking that was the best thing. If you'd said the water had been out, or that we were hammered with people coming in, she would have headed back immediately. Now, y'all head out. I'm going to finish up here." Becky Lee shot them all a don't-argue-with-me look.

The three women left and Becky Lee turned to the stack of dishes before her and sighed. Best start doing them if she wanted to get home before midnight.

CHAPTER 14

Hunt wrapped his arm loosely around Keely's thin
waist as they walked along a short, exposed part
of the shoreline. The beach here in the small inlet area
near Apalachicola, Florida was a mix of sand and silt,
not the fine white sand directly on the gulf. A small
shrimp boat tugged its way to a row of small piers on the
far side of the inlet. A blue heron walked along the
shoreline up ahead while sea gulls scattered as they
strolled along the water's edge. He paused every so often
to snap a quick photo as they walked. He caught an
image of Keely sitting on the edge of an old pier, where
the golden light of the sunset poured around her. He
took some photos of her looking out at the water,
dangling her feet back and forth. It seemed like she'd
gotten used to looking up and seeing Hunt with the
camera turned on her.

It had been a remarkable few days. Keely had come
alive as the hours slipped by, jotting notes, writing her

article. Each night they'd sort through his photos and read through the draft of her piece. Each night he'd briefly kissed her good night before she disappeared into her own motel room. Each night he'd walked the steps back to his own room, feeling a loneliness he hadn't felt since coming back to Comfort Crossing.

He'd gotten used to being on his own with his career and his travels, but now he had so many people back in his life—family, friends, and Keely, of course. He wasn't sure what he'd call Keely. Not really his girlfriend, but more than a friend.

Keely reached down and picked up a shell and tossed it into the water. The gulls squawked in complaint. She held out her hand for his and he took the small, sandy hand in his own.

"Want to go back to the B&B and have that bottle of wine we picked up?" Hunt didn't really want the evening to end.

"That sounds nice. It looks like it will get dark soon."

As they stood there on the beach, he couldn't help himself. He leaned down and kissed Keely gently. Her lips were warm and welcoming and she made a little sound in the back of her throat. She wrapped her arms around his neck. He deepened the kiss, sighed, then slowly pulled back.

"Um, what was that for?" Keely absentmindedly ran her finger over her lips.

"Just wanted a kiss. That's all." He wanted a kiss and so much more with this woman. But he'd nothing to offer. He had no home, and his only job was roaming the world taking his photos. But for now—now he wanted her kisses. Her hand in his. Her smiles she flashed his direction.

They turned around and headed back towards the B&B. They'd found a cute B&B in a little white house across the street from the water. They wandered back to the house and rinsed their feet in a spigot near the front steps. Keely sat on the swing at the end of the porch while Hunt grabbed the bottle of wine from his room and snagged some wine glasses from the proprietor.

He paused when he got back to the screened front door. Keely sat in the porch swing, deep in thought. He stood watching her, wanting to stamp the image on his mind, like a cherished photograph. She looked up and smiled at him.

Yes, that smile. That's the smile he waited for, the one that kept him coming back for more.

He pushed on through the screen door and sat down beside her on the swing. He carefully poured them each a glass of wine, and leaned against the back of the swing, one arm draped around Keely's shoulder.

Keely liked the feeling of Hunt's arm around her. She liked his warmth seeping over to keep the chill away. They sat in companionable silence on the front porch. A gentle breeze drifted across from the water. For a while they just gently rocked back and forth in the swing and sipped their wine. Keely couldn't remember another living soul who she felt this comfortable with, who she could just sit with in silence and thoroughly enjoy herself. The night darkened around them with the random call of the gulls and an occasional car passing down the road, their headlights cutting a swath across the darkness until they faded into the distance.

"Another glass?" Hunt leaned over and picked up the wine bottle sitting on the weathered gray boards of the porch.

"Sure, that sounds good. Just a short one, though." Keely held out her glass while Hunt poured the rich mahogany-colored wine. She sipped on her drink and stared across at the beach in the moonlight. It was back to the real world tomorrow. It was time. She'd called Katherine every day, but her sister had assured her everything was fine. Keely was anxious to get back and see, if indeed, everything was as good as Katherine said.

"You look lost in thought. Thinking about the cafe?"

"How'd you guess?"

"We've been gone three days, and I figured that's about your limit."

"It is. But I've had a really great time. It was nice to get away. It was nice to write again. Thanks for going over my article this afternoon."

"I'll send it in when I send in my photos. I've already mentioned it to my editor."

"I can't thank you enough for doing this. Even if nothing comes out of it, it was fun to work with you again." Keely felt a longing inside, the familiar tug of wanting to be able to roam the world, write, and most of all, make her own choices. She sighed.

"That was a heartfelt sigh." Hunt took her hand in his.

The connection to him was electrifying, comforting, and yet, unnerving.

"What's wrong?" He squeezed her hand.

She paused for a moment, trying to put her feelings into words. So many emotions had bubbled through her the last few days. Freedom. Guilt. Happiness. Regret. "I just feel… lost. Trapped. Wondering when I'll ever have a time away again like this." A *magical* time like this.

At that very moment, it hit her. It hit her hard, with a quickening of breath and a whirl of why-didn't-I-see-it-before-this thoughts. It was not only the excitement of traveling and writing. It was spending time with Hunt. That was a big part of what had made it so extraordinary. His smiles, his teasing, a random kiss here and there. Talking, lots of talking. Just sitting here holding his hand. She would miss all of this. Tomorrow was the end of a truly enchanting time for her. Yet she had to go back. She had to.

Hunt gently rocked the swing with one stretched out foot. "I sound like a broken record, but maybe it's time to let Katherine run the cafe for a bit. Take some time to travel. Maybe go back to school. Night school might be possible. It seems like Katherine is handling things okay this week. With a bit more time to learn the ropes, she could probably do just fine. I know you said no before, but now that Katherine is catching on to things, don't you think you could just do some things for yourself?"

And just like that, the mood was broken, shattered

into a million if onlys. Keely could physically feel the magic slipping away into the night, out of her reach, never to be grasped again. Hunt sat clueless to the obliteration of the hypnotic charm that had been hers for just a brief few days.

"I just can't dump the cafe on Katherine. It wouldn't be right." Keely's chest tightened and the familiar wave of guilt washed over her, crushing her in its magnitude. It was all her fault. Everything. There was no way she'd leave Kat to deal with the cafe, not to mention their mother. She couldn't. Not now, not ever.

"I know I've said it before, but everyone has a right to make the kind of life they want for themselves. Make choices. Live their life how they want to. You just need to look at Katherine as the grown woman she has become. And you know what? She seems to love working at the cafe. It should be a win, win situation for both of you."

"I can't just run off and leave Katherine. I can't leave her with the cafe or leave her to deal with Mother." Keely's voice was low and she struggled to control the tears that threatened to flow.

"I just don't understand." Hunt looked at her with an expression that clearly said he thought she was wrong.

But then, Hunt didn't know the truth, the whole truth. Oh, he knew it was her fault her father had had a heart attack—not that he agreed with her. But he didn't know Katherine's accident was all her fault. Her mother knew, though, and had never let an opportunity go by where she didn't subtly hint at it.

Keely swallowed and turned to look at Hunt. He would never look at her the same after she told him the truth, but she was going to try to explain.

"I'll explain, but you have to promise you won't tell anyone. I can't bear to have anyone else know."

"I promise."

It had all been such a petty argument, that night so long ago.

Keely took a deep breath to try to make him understand why she had to stay, had to run the cafe, had to take care of everything. She'd never told another person the truth, though her mother knew it and never let her forget it. "You see…" Keely cleared her throat and continued, "Katherine's accident was all my fault."

Hunt's eyes went wide, and he sat up straight, bringing the swing to an abrupt halt. "What do you mean it was your fault?"

"Kat wanted to borrow my car the night of the accident. You know the one I saved up for to take to college? Well, I was mad because she'd borrowed a red sweater of mine the night before without asking and left it on the floor with a chocolate malt stain on it. A stupid, stupid sweater." Keely looked out into the night, away from Hunt's eyes. She couldn't bear to see the coming disillusionment in his eyes. She couldn't bear for Hunt to look at her like her mother did.

"She asked to borrow my car that night because she had the hardest time driving my father's stick shift car. Mine was automatic. But since I was mad at her, I said no. It wasn't that I was going to use it, I was actually just working that night, but I said no. So, she convinced

159

Father to let her use his car. Off she went in a car she could barely manage. All because of a stupid sweater and a senseless fight. You know the rest. She lost control of the car, probably when she tried to shift gears going around that curve. If I had just let her use my car, none of this would have happened." Keely took a deep breath, still deliberately looking away from Hunt, putting up a wall of defense.

"My mother heard our argument, and will never let me forget the accident could have been prevented if I just hadn't been so selfish. She blames me for my father's heart attack, too. I can hardly fault her for her attitude towards me. Between my not letting Kat borrow my car, and causing my father's heart attack, I have ruined my family. I am such a disappointment to my mother. I'm a disappointment to myself. I'll work the rest of my life to make it up to Katherine and Mother, if it's the last thing I do. I owe them that much, and so much more."

The guilt still had the power to stab her to the bone, so acute it was a physical pain. The tears came now, in a hot rush, blinding her. She didn't even bother to swipe them away. No amount of tears would be able to wash away her guilt. She was a terrible sister, a horrible daughter, and the least she could do was run the cafe and try to keep the family afloat financially—and she wasn't doing a very good job of that, either.

She turned to look at Hunt, knowing she'd see the disillusionment in his eyes. Instead, she saw a hint of pain, and the twinge of guilt. She recognized guilt, she could spot it from a mile away.

~

A rush of guilt pounded through Hunt. All these years Keely had been blaming herself for Katherine's accident... and now, he knew the truth but was sworn to secrecy. A wave of anguish rolled over him, torn between his promise to his sister, and this woman sitting beside him, crushed by her guilt. His heart pounded in his chest and the feeling Keely had just been saying she had? Of being trapped? That's exactly how he felt at this very minute.

He wanted to take her into his arms and tell her nothing was her fault, that she didn't have to keep living with the guilt. He wanted to take that haunted look from her sad eyes and wipe away the tears making tracks down her cheek. He wanted to tell her the accident had been Kevin's fault. Kevin, who would surely have told Keely, if he'd known that she thought it was her fault.

Right?

Or would he? He'd kept it a secret until his deathbed, swearing Natalie to silence.

Hunt couldn't break his promise to his sister, couldn't go against Kevin's wishes, but he couldn't stand there and see Keely in such pain.

He stood up, pulled Keely to her feet, and wrapped his arms around her, holding her close. His shirt dampened from her tears, and he patted her back awkwardly, cursing the position he'd been put in with his promise to Natalie.

"I don't think all this is your fault, Keely." He stroked her hair. "Accidents happen. People have heart attacks. You can't live your life out of some kind of assumed guilt."

"You don't understand. You've never taken on any responsibility. You've always just done what you want."

Her words were like a punch in the gut. But she had no way of knowing. He'd kept his private life hidden when they were in high school, so she'd no way of knowing how hard he'd tried to take on responsibility.

Responsibility that he'd been more than willing accept, but the outcome had been disastrous. His thoughts drifted to his failures with his mother, his sister, the young photojournalist who died under his watch...

"I haven't always done just what I wanted and had things go my way." He kept his voice low and controlled. But now was not the time to get into that. Now was the time to make Keely feel better.

"You keep saying I have a choice, but I have no choice. None. It's my duty."

He tilted her chin up so he could see her eyes. "Ah, if I could only take away your pain and your guilt." He could take away some of it if he only told her the truth. But he wasn't going to break a promise to his sister. He couldn't.

But he sure could talk to Natalie first thing after they got back. She would understand. She would let him tell Keely what had really happened... unless she couldn't stand to let people think badly of Kevin now that he was gone.

He let out a long breath of air. How the heck was he

going to convince Natalie without breaking his promise to keep Keely's secret?

He gritted his teeth. He should stop making stupid promises, that's for sure.

Keely's phone rang, and she dashed away her tears. She pulled away from him and dug the phone out of her pocket. She glanced at the front of the phone and her eyes widened. "Kat? Everything okay?"

Keely turned her back to him. "Are you okay? Is everyone okay? Who was there? How did it happen?"

Hunt strained to hear the other side of the conversation.

"Did a doctor check you out?" Keely strode up and down the porch as she talked. "I think we can be there in about six hours if we leave now."

Hunt glanced at his watch. It was late, whatever happened must be bad for Keely to want to start back at this time of night.

"Everything okay?" Hunt mouthed the words. Keely shook her head no.

"Are you sure? We can leave right now." Keely stopped pacing and turned. "Okay, we'll leave first thing in the morning, I promise. Get some rest."

Keely clicked off the phone and whirled to face him, her eyes flashing and an I-told-you-so look firmly plastered on her face. "See? I told you... I told *everyone* that I shouldn't leave. There was a fire tonight at the cafe."

CHAPTER 15

T hey drove the six hours back to Comfort Crossing mostly in silence. Keely had insisted they start out at first light, no breakfast, only a quick stop for gas and coffee. The tension grew between them as the miles rolled away, filling the truck with a stifling, choking pressure. He tried taking Keely's hand, but she pulled it back and set it in her lap. She sat silently, staring out the window, probably blaming him and berating herself for ever leaving Katherine to run the cafe.

By the time they hit the town limits of Comfort Crossing, his stomach was growling and his mind was a roller coaster, dipping and swirling with thoughts of how to help Keely. He'd hoped that taking her away for a brief trip would help, but now it appeared it had only reinforced her opinion she should never leave town.

"Drop me at the cafe, will you?" Keely still didn't look at him.

He found a parking space on Main Street near the

cafe and Keely hopped out. "I'll get my things later." She shoved the truck door closed and hurried into the cafe.

He slid out of the truck and followed her, not sure what they would find. He pushed open the door and stepped inside, momentarily surprised that the normally cheerful brightness of the cafe was replaced by a murky darkness.

Ah, the electricity was turned off, and the windows were covered with soot.

Keely was leaning down, her arms wrapped around Katherine. Natalie came rushing up to him and gave him a quick hug.

"You okay, sis?"

"Yes, I'm fine."

"What happened?"

"The fire chief said he thinks it was an electrical problem. Started in the back by the door to the patio. Lots of smoke. It smells horrible in here, doesn't it?"

"Yep. Pretty smoky smelling. Who's that?" He nodded toward a man with a notebook near the doors to the patio.

"Insurance guy. Checking things out. Katherine called the insurance company first thing this morning."

"When did this happen?"

"At the end of the dinner rush, so we didn't have many customers. They all got out quickly. Had a bit of a scare with Kat, though. She got burned when she tried to smother the first of the flames. Luckily Becky Lee was near and grabbed the fire extinguisher. Got the fire out in no time."

Hunt glanced over at Katherine and saw that her

arm was wrapped from wrist to elbow in white bandages. Keely's mother hovered over Katherine. He could hear Mrs. Granger's voice rise as she talked to Keely.

He finally couldn't take it any longer and strode over to where Keely stood. He couldn't dampen his urge to protect her.

"I told you this was all too much for Katherine. Look at the burn on her arm." Mrs. Granger flung her arm and pointed her finger. "You were off lollygagging around with that Robichaux boy, and Katherine was here working herself to exhaustion."

"Mother. None of this is Keely's fault. It was an electrical fire. It could have happened when she was here," Katherine intervened.

Hunt stood silently at Keely's side, not wanting to enter into the family argument, but willing Keely to feel his strength.

"No, Mother is right. I should have never left you alone. It was too much. You do look exhausted."

"That's because I spent hours in the emergency room while they gave me this ridiculously large bandage for a minor burn. I'm really okay."

"What if it had been worse? What if Katherine would have been trapped in here with the fire?" Mrs. Granger's voice edged on hysteria now, laced with a burning anger. "I asked you not to leave."

Keely wasn't sure if her mother was talking about her

leaving to go out of town with Hunt, or her leaving for class all those years ago when her father had his heart attack. Either way, her mother was right. She should have stayed.

"Mother, I'm sorry." Her mother was never going to forgive her. Not for then. Not for now. A hurt, so deep in her soul that it felt like she was never going to recover, flowed through her.

"You should be sorry. It was so irresponsible and selfish of you."

Keely blinked back tears, clinching her fists at her side. "It was. I'm sorry. I'll get this all sorted out."

"Hey, I'm sitting right here." Katherine's voice rang out strong and angry. "I was doing a fine job running the cafe. I've called the insurance company. A recovery company is due any minute to work on getting the smoke smell out. I've called the electrician and the county inspector. They've found the electrical problem. We'll get it fixed and be back open in a few days, a week tops."

Keely went from reeling from her mother's attack—though it was justified—to looking at Kat in amazement. "You did all of that already?"

"You bet I did. I am capable, quit acting like I'm not. I know you took over everything after my accident and after Father died, but I'm here to help now. Let me."

"I still say that this is too much for you Katherine, dear." Her mother bent down and patted Katherine's shoulder. Her sister stiffened and reached up to take her mother's hand off her shoulder.

"No, Mother, it's not. We're going to reopen. We're

going to get the patio opened and ready for Summerfest, and with any luck we'll have our most successful summer ever."

Katherine took Keely's hand. "Together. We'll do that together."

Just then the inspector came walking up, tapping his pen on his notebook. "I see you're doing some construction out back."

"We're adding a patio area, yes." Keely looked at the man.

"Mess with any electricity while building it?"

"No, sir." Hunt stepped up. "I had all the utilities flagged before I started. The electrical work is already hired out to a certified electrician, but he hasn't even started on it yet. He's scheduled to start this week."

"Well, a bit coincidental that the fire starting in the back wall with the construction going on."

Keely's heart plummeted. What if the insurance company didn't cover the damage? How could they recover the costs to repair the damage? They'd have to postpone their plans for the patio. Then they would be right back where they were now. Without enough space. No waiting room. Locked in a downward spiral.

Kat rolled up to face the man. "I have the inspector's report in a file in the office. He looked at the area before he gave us the building permit. You'll see that he didn't find anything wrong, and that the utilities were flagged." Katherine looked up at the man defiantly.

"I just might need those records, little lady."

"Excuse me?" Keely faced the insurance man, hands

on her hips. "Little Lady? I think you meant Miss Granger."

The man didn't even have the decency to look sheepish. "Yeah, sure. The records?"

"I'll get them." Katherine wheeled away toward the office.

"Tell you what. We'll get copies made and drop them by the insurance office. Wouldn't want to give you our only copy. Wouldn't want it getting lost." It might not be the smartest thing to anger the insurance guy, but he really was an insufferable fool. Keely stood with her hands on her hips, facing the arrogant insurance man.

"I guess that would be okay."

"Good then. Here, I'll walk you out." Keely headed to the door with the we-don't-really-want-to-pay -your-claim man in her wake.

She closed the door behind him and looked around the cafe. There were black, sooty marks on the back wall and the ceiling above. The whole cafe smelled like a leftover campfire, a campfire where the campers had burned something terribly.

The weight of the work ahead of them came crashing down on her. The clean up. Getting the patio ready. All this by Summerfest. She looked over at Kat talking to Natalie and Hunt. Thank goodness her sister hadn't been badly hurt, and all the customers had gotten out safely.

Just then the door opened and in walked Camille with Delbert.

"Keely, hon. I heard the horrible news about the diner. A fire. Was it a grease fire? That's just so terrible. I guess you'll be closed for a while now, won't you? Looks like Delbert and I won't have a chance to eat here on this trip to town."

What a shame.

Camille turned her back on Keely and traipsed over to Kat. "Katherine, you poor dear. Are you okay? Word around town is that you got burned. Oh, my. Look at your arm. It must have been frightening to be trapped in here in that wheelchair."

Last nerve. The woman was sitting on her last nerve. Keely strode over to her sister, her shoes clicking determinedly on the vinyl flooring.

"Camille. Why it is so good to see you. Thank you *so* much for your concern." Katherine practically simpered.

But Keely recognized the look in her sister's eyes.

"And this must be Delbert. I've heard so much about him. Hamilton. Of the Hamilton hotel chain." Sarcasm ran through her sister's voice, but Camille was so self-involved she missed it.

Camille then turned to Hunt and flashed on her belle-of-the-ball charm. "Hunt. How nice to see you. You're looking good. What brings you back here? I would think the town would bore you to tears now."

"Ah, Camille. You haven't changed a bit." Hunt leaned back on the counter, putting distance between himself and Camille.

"Oh, that's sweet." Camille preened a bit.

Katherine looked over at Keely and rolled her eyes. Natalie smothered a grin.

"Hunt, you really should join Delbert and me for a nice dinner at Sylvia's Place. Have a *good* meal. We'd love to hear all about your travels. We're planning a trip to Europe and could use tips on places to see. I know you've been just about everywhere in the world, haven't you?"

Delbert didn't look like he was very thrilled about the idea. He walked closer to Camille and put his hand on her arm with an air of possession. He probably spent half his time trying to keep Camille happy. If not more. Camille was the biggest flirt Keely had ever met.

"I'm pretty busy this trip." Hunt lounged against the counter, one long leg stretched out in front of him.

"Well, if you change your mind, you know where to reach me. I'm staying at Mama's house. I'm sure you still have the number, right?"

"Can't say that I ever did."

"Oh, don't be silly. You don't have to hide anything from Delbert. I already told him how we dated in high school."

"Wh—What?" Hunt looked like he was choking.

"Ta-ta. We better run along. Good luck cleaning the diner, Keely."

With the swirl of her skirt, she flounced out of the cafe, Delbert scurrying to keep up with her.

"I did what? She thinks we dated in high school? I never. I mean, seriously. Never." Hunt's face turned apoplectic, full of indignation.

Natalie laughed. "She always was good at revising history. Twisting things to suit her mood."

"But I never dated her. Ever."

"If you say so, brother dear."

"Well, Poor-Katherine-Dear is going to go call the

food vendors and hold off on the deliveries for a few days." Katherine grinned at herself.

Mrs. Granger turned to Keely. "I'm going to go home now. It's been such a frightful few days. I assume you'll handle things now and send Katherine home where she belongs?"

"Kat, mother is right. I'll handle things here. You go home and get some rest."

"Come along, Katherine." Her mother turned towards the door. "And you'll deal with all this mess, right?"

"Mom, I'm okay." Katherine tried to argue with their mother.

"Kat, you've been up all night. You got burned for goodness sakes. Go home. I've got this." She should have been here when it happened. Maybe she could have prevented Kat from being hurt. Anyway, it was her responsibility.

Keely watched her mother and Kat leave, then looked around the cafe. It was hard to believe that just yesterday she'd been away, free, having the time of her life. Now the real world had a death grip on her, punishing her for thinking she could escape, if only for a few days.

CHAPTER 16

"Natalie, we have to talk." Hunt had waited patiently for his sister to get the boys to bed.

"What about?" His sister dropped onto the sofa and picked up her knitting.

"About Kevin. His secret."

"I'd rather not talk about that again. I'm sorry you ever found that note. Kevin wanted the secret kept. He'd be mortified to know you found out." She set her knitting back down, a look of concern creased her face.

Hunt sat down on the sofa beside his sister and took her hand. "But I need to tell someone. It's important."

"You promised you'd keep the secret."

"I know. I wouldn't ask if it wasn't so important."

"Who do you want to tell?" Natalie grabbed a throw pillow and held it close.

Hunt sat up straight. "I… I can't tell you."

Natalie looked at him in amazement. "You want to

break your promise to me? Go against Kevin's wishes and you can't tell me why?"

Hunt's heart plummeted. The way Natalie made it sound, he was a scoundrel for even asking. But if he couldn't tell Keely, she was going to go on the rest of her life blaming herself.

"I can't explain, but someone needs to know."

"I can't bear to have anyone think badly of Kevin now that he's... gone." Natalie's voice was choked with tears. "He tried so hard to make things right. To help the Grangers. He was so young when it happened. You know, he even paid off some of Katherine's rehab bills. They never knew anything except that they had an anonymous donor."

Natalie jumped up, the pillow falling to the floor. "And I can't have the boys hearing about it. What if someone lets something slip? They are too young to understand." She turned to face him. "I just can't let you tell anyone."

"Natalie, it's so... important."

"I can't believe you'd even ask me this. I don't know what to say to you, Hunt. But, no. I have to respect Kevin's wishes."

"Kevin would probably want you to tell if he knew what I know."

"Hunt, you're talking in circles. No. I can't. You can't. Just, no." Natalie turned and slowly walked away and he heard her steps on the stairs.

Hunt reached down and scooped up the pillow Natalie had dropped on the floor. He could understand Natalie's point, and Kevin's secret wasn't his to tell.

Keely's guilt wasn't his to tell. He closed his eyes and took a long deep breath. How was he going to fix this mess?

Hunt wiped the sweat from his brow and wished for the bazillionth time the garage got some kind of cross breeze. He'd finished up the tabletops for the patio and he was attaching legs to each one, carefully making sure the tables were level.

He was racing against time to get everything ready for Keely's grand opening of the patio. Nothing was turning out as planned. He hadn't gotten enough matching pavers and had been unable to locate any more halfway through the project, so he'd gone with an alternating pattern around the edge. Keely said it was fine, but he chastised himself for not figuring out a better way, or even pulling the old pavers and alternating the whole patio. But there hadn't been time.

Then, the inspectors were all over the electrician since the fire. Justifiably so, he could grudgingly admit, but it caused even more delays. Plus, it hung in the air that the electrical problems had occurred after he'd started working on the patio. He racked his brain trying to think if he'd done anything that could have caused it. He couldn't think of anything, but he still felt like the inspector, and possibly Keely, thought it was coincidental that the electrical fire started after he'd begun work on the patio.

Working in the quiet garage was giving him too

much time to think. He stood upright, placed a hand on his lower back and arched, stretching to work out the kinks.

Natalie walked into the garage carrying a huge glass of tea. "Thought you could use this. And a peace offering. You still mad at me from last night? For asking you not to tell Kevin's secret?"

"I'm not mad. I wish you'd change your mind, but it's your decision." For now he was just going to let the subject rest. He walked over to Natalie and took the glass she extended to him. He took a big swig of the tea. "Ah, that's good. Thanks."

Natalie walked over and inspected a couple of the tables. "You just about finished with these?"

"Just a few more need legs, then I'm done."

"Keely will love them. They look really great."

"Now if the paddle fans I ordered would come in so we could get the electrician back out to install them before the opening..."

"The back order isn't your fault."

"Well, I keep trying to tell myself that, over and over. The mismatched pavers aren't my fault. The missing fans aren't my fault. I don't know why anyone ever decides to depend on me for... anything. Things just don't ever turn out the way people want them to if they leave me in charge." Hunt set the glass down with a little too much force, unable to chase away the nagging doubts he had that he'd get the patio finished in time.

"Hunt, you know, for years you've been hiding out. Afraid to let people close. Afraid to let anyone depend on you. At some point, you're going to have to realize it wasn't your fault Mama died. Wasn't your fault I was shipped off to Hattiesburg. Or, you can just spend the rest of your life running away. We all make choices."

With that, his sister headed back to the house. He swallowed hard and grimaced. His sister had always been able to get right to the heart of things, and pinpoint things just like they were.

He really admired that about her… except when she turned it on him.

CHAPTER 17

The electrician who did the wiring for the patio knocked once on the doorframe to Keely's office. "Got a minute?"

"Sure. What's up?"

"I hate to bother you, but the check you sent? It... bounced."

"What?" Keely sat up straight in her chair. "It couldn't have. I have the funds in the account. There must be some mess up at the bank."

"I figured that was it." But somehow he didn't look convinced.

"Let me call the bank, and I'll get back with you this afternoon. I'm sure I can sort this out."

"Okay, just let me know." The electrician tipped his cap and walked away.

Keely shoved aside the folders she was working on and dug out the direct phone number of the bank manager who always helped her. One more advantage of a small town, they knew her at the bank by name.

The manger answered on the third ring. "First Mississippi Bank. May I help you?"

"Hi. It's Keely over at the Magnolia Cafe."

Keely didn't miss the long pause before she got a response.

"Hi, Keely."

"The electrician was in here. Said his check bounced. Not possible. I deposited more than enough funds to cover it."

"I'm sorry, Keely." The bank manager's voice crackled through the phone line. "Your mother came in and transferred funds out of that account and set up a new one. So any outstanding checks will have insufficient funds. She said something about a security issue on the old account number."

Keely silently counted to three. Then to five. "I see." Six. Seven. Eight… *the heck with that.* "I don't suppose she added me to the new account?"

"She is the only signatory on it."

"Well, thank you for your time." Keely clicked down the phone in her office and pushed away from the desk. She paced back and forth in her cramped office.

The change of account surprised her, but then it didn't. Her mother had been upset ever since her world was rocked with Katherine starting to work at the cafe and the building of the patio area, not to mention the liquor license.

Keely stopped in her tracks.

Had her mother messed with the license too?

A wave of frustration washed over her. She was doing everything in her power to make the cafe a financial success, while her mother was firmly entrenched in the past, wanting nothing to change. The problem with that was, if they didn't change, the cafe wasn't going to make it.

Keely stuck her head out of her office. "Becky Lee, has my mother been by?"

"Haven't seen her."

"Okay. I have to run out for a few minutes. I'll be back."

Becky Lee nodded and flipped a brief wave.

Keely looked out the back door. No sign of Hunt. Which was good. And bad. She knew he'd been trying to talk to her, but she just didn't have the energy. She ducked out the back way, across the almost finished patio. No tables yet because the edge of the patio wasn't finished. She hoped Hunt had this all figured out, although it appeared that at this moment she didn't have access to any funds to pay him…

"Mother." Keely pushed through the front door of their house.

Her mother sat on the couch working on a crossword puzzle, pretending she hadn't just pulled the rug out from under Keely. "Hello, Keely."

"Seriously, Mother. You pull all the money out of

the account without telling me? Did you even think of the consequences? Checks to vendors bouncing? Messing with our shaky credit?"

"I think I would like to look over all expenditures now before they are paid."

"Really? That's where we are now? I've spent my whole life running the cafe for you, trying to make it profitable, working every single day. This is how you want to play it now?"

"I just don't think you girls are making good decisions."

"Which ones? Katherine helping with the bookwork? The patio? The few updates we've done to the inside? Getting a liquor license… we are getting that aren't we? You haven't messed with that, have you?" Keely's heart pounded in her chest.

"I don't see why we need to become a bar."

"We aren't becoming a *bar*." Keely wanted to stomp her feet and throw a tantrum like a two year old. Her mother was going to drive her right over the edge. Not that she'd a very good grip on that edge anyway these days.

"Well, I don't like to encourage that kind of thing."

"Mother, you have a glass of wine with dinner almost every night."

"Yes, well, that's in my own home."

Keely stood at the end of the couch, uncertain what to even say to this woman. She would never understand her mother, much less be close to her. Her mother was a total enigma.

"I don't like the changes you're making. Things are fine the way they are. You are just wasting money."

"Things aren't fine how they are. We're barely making ends meet. People are leaving because there is no place to wait if our tables are full. Which they are on the weekends, so we're just throwing business away. If they have a nice place to wait, or a place to go sit and have a glass of wine after dinner? That's a good thing. I've kept to a strict budget."

"You don't have enough help as it is."

"If business picks up, I'll be able to hire the help I need."

"I just think I should be back making the decisions."

"Mother, you haven't been involved in the day to day running of the cafe for over fifteen years. I've been running it. Doing everything possible to keep it afloat." Keely stopped and looked at her mother. "But nothing I do will ever be good enough for you will it? You'll never forgive me. Never be proud of me."

"I don't know what you're talking about."

"You blame me for Dad's heart attack. You blame me for Kat's accident. I can't ever make that right for you."

Her mother looked down at her crossword for a brief moment, then back up to meet Keely's eyes. "You did play your part in destroying the wonderful life we had. If you hadn't left to go to that class, maybe everything would have been different."

"Mother." Katherine rolled out of her room and crossed over to the couch. "You didn't just blame Keely for Father's heart attack."

185

KAY CORRELL

"If she wouldn't have insisted she needed to go to that class. Put herself first."

"How about if Dad had taken the medicine he'd been prescribed for his high blood pressure? Changed his diet like the doctor said? Started exercising. Don't you think that's where the responsibility lies?" Katherine swung her chair to face their mother.

"What are you talking about?" Keely was at a loss.

"Father. He'd been to the doctor and knew he had high blood pressure. High cholesterol. He'd been put on a diet. Told to exercise. Didn't you know this?"

"I had no idea."

"Well, I did. Mother did. You were so busy with trying to keep the cafe going when I got hurt, that you were barely at home. But, yes, Father was told to do all that. I even nagged him to take his meds, but he just... didn't."

"Your father didn't like to take medicine. Never did."

"Well, Mother, *that* is what killed Father. Not Keely going to class. He chose not to listen to his doctor. He chose not to take his medicine. His choice. He left us behind because of those choices."

"Katherine, I will not have you blaming your father."

"But, I do." Katherine's voice was low. "I miss him so much. He could have had a chance to be here with us. I just don't understand his choices."

Keely's mother stood up. "I will not have you talking about him like that. Show him some respect. This is why I'm taking back control. Keely needs someone to... restrain her."

186

Keely gritted her teeth. Someone to *restrain* her. All she'd ever done is give her all to Magnolia Cafe.

Her mother's footsteps echoed down the hall, and she braced against the inevitable almost door slam that her mother had perfected.

Keely sank to the couch, reeling from her mother's words, and struggling to absorb all her sister had said. Her father had known he had heart disease. He'd known it. And ignored it. She remembered how he never took an aspirin for a headache or back pain. Refused to take antibiotics. Gutted his way through any illness. But sometimes medicine could save your life...

"What was Mom talking about? Taking back control?" Katherine transferred from her wheelchair to the couch.

Keely didn't want to burden Katherine with the mess.

"You need to tell me."

Keely sighed. "She transferred all the cafe money to a new account. I don't sign on it. She wants to okay everything we spend."

"She didn't."

"Ah, but she did. The check to the electrician bounced. I assume I'll get calls very soon from our suppliers. I need to look and see what's outstanding on the account."

"Oh, I'm so sorry. I knew that she was upset. She doesn't do change well."

"Really? You noticed that?" Keely forced a weak smile. "And she needs to *restrain* me." She was used to the feeling she'd never win her mother's approval, but this last move of her mother's stuck a nerve deep inside, a hurt she tried to keep hidden, even from herself.

"You know, you could just walk away from it all. Let her deal with the consequences." Katherine shifted on the couch.

"I can't do that. If it fails you'll have nothing for your future."

"I can work. I can find a job."

"We can't just let her ruin the family business."

"But, the cafe isn't your dream, anyway."

"No, it isn't, but it's my responsibility."

Katherine took her hand. "No, Keely, it isn't. It was Mother and Father's responsibility. Mother could have helped, but she just left it all to you to figure out. You've spent years keeping things running. I want to help you now. You need to let me help you now."

Keely looked at her sister, at the woman she'd become. The strong woman. The capable woman. Keely sighed. "I have a hard time accepting help after all this time of going it alone."

Katherine squeezed her hand. "I know you do. You've been fighting giving me things to do, ever since the fire."

"I have. I know that. It's just you could have been hurt worse than you were. I felt like I shouldn't have left you."

"It's not your fault Dad had a heart attack, and it's not your fault there was a fire when you went away for a few days. You need to let it go. Move on. Let me help you."

Tears brimmed in her eyes. "I could use help. I'm so

worn out. Tired of arguing with Mother. Tired of working every single day."

"So, first things first. We need to find a way to get Mother to let you sign checks again."

"How do you think we'll ever get that to happen?"

"I'll think of something."

CHAPTER 18

Izzy closed her notebook, the last item on the list checked off. "I think we have it all set."

"You have it all set. I don't know how we would have pulled off this wedding without you." Jenny pushed back from the table at the Magnolia Cafe.

"I love to organize events. You know that."

Izzy sat at a table at the Magnolia cafe and drummed her fingers on the table. Jenny looked at her friend and smiled. Izzy always did that when she was deep in thought, sorting something out. Jenny leaned back and sipped her sweet tea, waiting for Becky Lee to finish up her shift. They were meeting to iron out the last of the wedding details. Jenny's stomach fluttered when she realized it was less than two weeks away. All these years and she was finally going to become Clay's wife.

Though, she still couldn't shake the uneasy feeling that had been swirling around her all spring.

Becky Lee plopped down beside Jenny with a large

slice of chocolate cake and three forks. "Thought we could use a bit of reinforcement. Don't tell your kids you had dessert before dinner."

"Sworn to secrecy." Jenny smiled.

"So, do we—and by we, I mean Izzy—have everything all set for the wedding?" Becky Lee nodded toward the notebook in on the table.

"I think *we* do." Izzy grinned and dug her fork into a bite of the cake. "Now, if I can just finish up my to-do list for Summerfest, it will all be good."

"Hey, did you guys hear there's a hurricane forming out in the Atlantic?" Becky Lee leaned against the table.

"No. Isn't it kind of early for that?" Izzy's face creased in concern. "I hope it doesn't dump a bunch of rain on us. We have Summerfest and the wedding coming up."

A shiver ran up Jenny's spine. "I'm sure it will just dissipate, right? I mean it's too early for a big storm."

"I can come up with a backup plan for the wedding, but a big storm will sure put the brakes on Summerfest. If a hurricane gets forecasted for this area, we'll lose all the tourist traffic we were counting on." Izzy sighed. "I'll just will the darn thing away. I've put too much effort into Summerfest for it to be ruined by a hurricane."

"I think that even a hurricane won't argue with Izzy when she has her mind set. I'm sure the storm is breaking up as we speak," Becky Lee assured her friend.

"What other news do you have?" Jenny knew Becky Lee always was the first to know anything, with her Magnolia Cafe pipeline to town news.

"Well, Keely is still working on the liquor license for

the cafe. She's hoping it comes through any day. Y'all will have to come to the grand opening of the patio. She's having it the day before Summerfest starts, if Hunt gets the final things finished out here. He seems a bit worried."

"Clay and I will come." Jenny made a mental note to tell Clay about it.

Izzy, of course, made an actual note in her notebook. "I'll have to check with Owen. He swears he'll be in town for Summerfest, but I'm not sure when he's actually going to get here."

"Well, I'm hoping the patio area with the wine bar will help out the Magnolia Cafe financially. I know Keely is always struggling to keep things going. Hopefully Summerfest will be a boon for business, too. Closing down for that week after the fire hit them kind of hard, but at least the whole place got a fresh coat of paint, and Natalie's ideas for the patio have turned out great."

"I hope it works out for Keely. Heck, I hope Summerfest helps to bring in business to my shop."

"Jenny, what's up? You have that lost-in-space thing going on."

Becky Lee interrupted Jenny's thoughts, and she realized she'd only been half-listening.

"I'm not sure. I just have this strange feeling about the wedding."

"Butterflies. All brides have them." Becky Lee spoke like she was an authority, not a confirmed single woman.

"Yes, you're probably right. I'm just being silly." Jenny pushed away from the table. "Well, I better go.

Greta is making dinner for all of us tonight, and I want to get there and help her out."

Jenny walked away from her friends after assuring them everything was all right. Only… she still didn't think everything *was* all right.

~

Keely looked around the cafe. Less than a week until the grand opening of the patio. Her mother had looked at every single bill that came in, second guessing everything, but Keely had gritted her teeth and carried on with the running of the cafe. Her mother had put a stop on spending anything else on renovating the patio or updating the cafe. Keely had actually paid the electrician and Hunt out of some meager savings she had.

Keely walked over to the antique hutch and adjusted the basket of menus. A long church pew had been cleaned up, polished, and sat in front of the row of windows. Surely her mother could see how nice the cafe looked now with just the few changes? Maybe if business picked up, her mother would even be proud of her. Maybe her mother would acknowledge all Keely had done to make the cafe a financial success.

Maybe.

"Keely, you want to come see this?" Hunt walked up behind her. "I brought over all the tables and have them out on the patio. You can let me know if you want me to rearrange them."

Keely turned to look at Hunt. She hadn't seen much

of him since their trip. He'd been busy with the patio and she'd been busy getting things ready for the patio opening and Summerfest.

Plus, she'd been avoiding him.

"Sure. I've been wanting to see how the tables turned out." She knew both Bella and Natalie thought this mismatched arrangement of tables and chairs would look great, but Keely could not picture it in her mind. But then, she wasn't really the decorating type. She was the grown woman who lived in her childhood room and had never so much as painted the walls. She hadn't thought to take down the posters she had up from her high school days until her late twenties. What did that say about her?

She followed Hunt out to the patio, pausing briefly to say hi to one of their customers. She pushed through the French doors and stepped outside.

"So? Do you like it?" Hunt's face had a boyish look of expectation.

She looked around, from table to table, with the quaint doors smooth from polyurethane for tabletops and an array of legs ranging from spindles to wrought iron, to pedestals. She ran her hand over the table nearest her. "Oh, it's wonderful. I never imagined it would look this nice. Each one is so different, but somehow they all tie in together."

"I think it looks great. Bella and Natalie had really creative ideas for out here. I still have a few more chairs to bring over, but you get the idea."

"I will never doubt anything Bella or Natalie says about decorating. Ever."

"I learned years ago to never doubt Natalie. On anything." Hunt grinned at her.

She refused to acknowledge the rush of emotion that flooded through her when he flashed that grin her direction.

"I'm still hoping the ceiling paddle fans come in before the opening, I'm really sorry they aren't here yet." Hunt scowled a bit.

She looked up at the ceiling, focusing on it, instead of Hunt standing there with his impossibly sexy tool belt riding low on his hips. "It's not really your fault they didn't come in. It hasn't been very warm yet. I think we'll be fine."

"Well, I promised to have it all finished by Summerfest."

"It's close enough, Hunt. You've done such a good job." She turned to look at him then. "So, I guess you're headed out after Summerfest?"

Hunt wanted to just stare at her and soak in the look of approval she'd given to everything about the patio. Instead, she'd brought up the elephant in the room. Summerfest. That had been his guideline for the last few months. He'd stay until Summerfest was over. But then what?

"I'm not quite sure what my plans are yet."

"Still waiting to see what assignment to take?" Keely tucked a wisp of hair behind her ear.

"Yes. I mean, no." Hunt stood there, helplessly. "I mean I don't have firm plans yet."

And by firm plans, he meant no plans at all.

He was so uncertain what to do next. Natalie was as independent as they came, and would never ask him to stay and help, but it was obvious she liked having him around. Even Jackson was starting to accept him instead of rolling his eyes at everything he did. He'd learned to make mac and cheese just like Jamie liked it. Jesse had taken an interest in photography, and Hunt had gotten him an inexpensive camera and they went on photo expeditions to the park and the beach.

To be honest, having those boys depend on him scared him more than a dangerous photo assignment in some god-forsaken land. What if he failed them? He should leave before they got really used to having him around.

Then there was Keely.

Or maybe there wasn't.

He didn't have any idea what they were any more. When they'd been on their trip, he'd been so sure they were more than friends, but the last few weeks they'd been... well, even less than friends.

He took a step, closed the distance between them and took her hand, half surprised she didn't snatch it away. "Keely, I don't know how we got so off track. I miss talking to you."

"There isn't much point, is there? You're leaving. I'm here trying to wrestle the cafe back from Mother before she ruins us, in order to secure a future for Kat and her. And me, I guess."

She was probably right, there wasn't much point. He wasn't sure why right that very moment it seemed like such a good idea to kiss her.

So he did.

~

Keely clung to Hunt's strong, solid arms as he kissed her, his lips firm yet gentle against hers. Her thoughts whirled. She'd promised herself she was going to stay away from him. It was silly to be standing here kissing a man who was leaving any day. But then, the kiss was just so delightful.

Hunt pulled away slowly. "I've been wanting to do that for days. Weeks." His voice was low and growly.

"It was… nice."

"Nice? You thought that was *nice*? I thought it was great. Better than great. I could spend half my day kissing you and it wouldn't be enough." He tightened his arms around her.

She leaned against him, unable to resist. She rested her cheek against his worn work shirt, listening to his heart thumping in his chest.

Okay, he was right, that kiss was fireworks and lightning good.

"Here, let's try it again." Hunt leaned down and kissed her. Slowly and thoroughly. Gently but demandingly.

Not that he was asking anything she wasn't more than willing to give. She clutched his shirt in her hands, steadying herself. She lost all her reasons why it was a bad idea to kiss this man.

He pulled away slightly, one arm still wrapped around her waist. "Now, was that *nice*?"

"You win. It was…" She stopped to pull her thoughts together. "It was perfect."

Hunt stood with a self-satisfied grin plastered across his chiseled face. "Perfect is so much better than nice."

CHAPTER 19

B ella punched up the weather on her laptop. It looked like the hurricane was turning a bit and would miss coming their way. It had slowed down some, too. So even if it brought storms, Summerfest should still be a go. Then she just had to worry about the weather for Jenny's wedding.

She glanced up when she heard someone knock. "Owen. You're here." She jumped up from the kitchen table and opened the screen door. He wrapped his arms around her and hugged her close.

"I wouldn't miss Summerfest. I told you that."

"I was getting worried that you wouldn't make it on time. It all starts tomorrow. Did you see that the hurricane has slowed down? We're going to have beautiful weather for the festival."

"I did hear the hurricane has stalled. I've been checking on it for days. Didn't want anything to ruin Summerfest for you."

They walked into the house, arm and arm. She poured some sweet tea, and they sat back down at the table, two large notebooks spread before her, one for Summerfest and one for Jenny's wedding.

"Now, what can I do to help? I'm here to do anything you need."

"I was getting ready to head over to Magnolia Cafe. It's the grand opening of Keely's patio area. Kind of the kickoff for Summerfest. Do you want to come with me?"

"Sure do. I plan on doing no business this weekend. I'm all yours."

"I like the sound of that. All mine." She smiled at him, glad to have him back in town, if only for a while.

"Where are the boys?"

"Ah, the quiet gave away that they aren't here, didn't it?" She laughed. "They're at their dad's for the night. So I guess I'm all yours."

Owen raised his eyebrows. "I like the sound of that."

Bella leaned over and gave Owen a quick kiss. "I've missed you."

"I've missed you, too. Hoping to stick around for quite a bit this time."

She knew he meant it... it just didn't seem to work out very often. He often planned for long trips back to Comfort Crossing, but it seemed like something always pulled him away. In spite of all of his promises that he'd be back for Summerfest, she hadn't really been sure until he walked in her door.

Owen put a hand on her knee. "I know that look."

"What look?"

"The doubting one. I'm really trying to be here more."

"I know you are. It's okay." Though she missed him so much when he was gone, it was hard to adjust when he was back in town, trying to fit in time with him along with taking care of the boys, running the shop, and whatever else she had going, like planning Jenny's wedding. It seemed like just when they got their footing again, off he'd go.

Owen reached over and traced one finger along the crease between her eyebrows. "I can hear you thinking."

She flashed a half smile.

"We're going to work things out, you'll see."

She hoped he was right.

He took both of her hands in his. "Bella, you know I'm crazy about you. I want this to work. I know it's hard on you when I'm gone so much. I want to be here for you. I do."

He leaned over and kissed her then, gently, raising one hand to cradle her face. She kissed him back, so glad this man was in her life, even if it was infrequently. She pulled away slightly, looked into his eyes, and smiled.

"I'm crazy about you, too."

Owen stood up abruptly, then took a few steps across the kitchen floor. She looked at him in surprise. He turned back towards her, then paused and looked directly in her eyes.

"I'm more than crazy about you, Bella. I should have been telling you every single day that I love you. Hopelessly and completely in love with you. I want something more for us than random dating on my trips to town."

She sat there staring at him wordlessly.

Maybe he'd spoken too soon. Maybe she wasn't ready for his words. He did have a habit of disappearing when least expected. He couldn't expect her to just... what? Get deeply involved with him when he always seemed to up and disappear. He wanted more with her, but he was so clueless about woman. Had no idea how she was going to react.

Now he'd just blurted out his feelings. Like a fool. Going in unprepared. That wasn't like him. He should have planned it out. Brought flowers, taken her to a romantic place. Not just thrown it out there in the middle of her kitchen.

He held his breath, his gaze locked on her face, waiting for her reaction.

"I... I wasn't expecting that..." Bella shifted in her chair.

His heart dropped in his chest. He'd rushed it. He was no good at relationships and had never felt this about anyone before. Someone ought to teach him remedial boyfriend or something.

He twisted his watch band, then stopped himself. His tell for nervousness. Don't let them see how you feel. He knew the rules. He'd broken them. He'd shown his hand.

He could hear the clock on the wall tick away the

seconds in the deadly quiet of the room. Each tick mocked him.

"Owen?"

"Um?" He swallowed, unable to speak.

"I love you, too. And yes, I'd like more than just dating when you come to town."

He could finally fill his lungs with air again. "You do? You would?" He could feel a foolish grin stretch across his face. "Really?"

"Really." She got up and came to stand right beside him. She reached up to touch his face. "I have for a long time. I was just waiting for you to catch up with me."

CHAPTER 20

Keely stood in the doorway of her office, looking out into the cafe. Four in the afternoon. The dinner crowd would start soon. She glanced through the French doors and saw the tables on the patio all decorated with flowers and candles. Natalie's idea.

Her mother had balked at the expense of flowers, of course, but Becky Lee had brought in cut flowers from her garden. They'd strung white Christmas lights along the railing surrounding the patio. The liquor license had come through, and they were stocked with a small selection of wines and beer.

She turned when she heard someone come into the cafe. Hunt. He was dressed in a nice button-down shirt and khaki slacks. She sucked in a quick breath when he flashed her his lopsided grin and winked at her.

He crossed the cafe in a few long strides, took a quick glance around, then kissed her. "That's for luck."

"Oh, that's a new thing? A kiss for luck?"

"Yep, everyone's doing it," Hunt teased.

"Then I guess it's okay." She smiled at him.

"You look a little nervous."

"I am. A bit. I just want everything to go well." She wanted everything to be fabulous, and her mother appreciate it. Acknowledge it. She'd tried so hard to make it up to her mother. Maybe this would be the night. She wanted her mother to smile at her and be proud of her. She craved it. Just this once. So she would know her mother had forgiven her.

Katherine and her mother came in the cafe at that very moment. Keely could feel herself holding her breath.

"Keely, everything looks great. There are fliers up around town about the opening. I bet we're really busy tonight." Katherine wheeled up to her. "Doesn't it look nice, Mother? Have you seen outside? The patio looks wonderful."

"Well, we'll see. Won't we?" Her mother glanced around the cafe. "The tables are awfully close together. Katherine can't make it through there, can she?"

"Mother, the tables are fine. I can get around fine."

"Well, I just came to drop off Katherine. She insisted she needed to be here. I'm headed home now."

With that, her mother turned and walked out the door, without so much as a glance at the patio and taking all of Keely's hopes of approval right out the door with her.

Keely stood behind the counter a few hours later and looked out over the cafe. The surprisingly empty cafe. A few tables of customers were scattered here and there, but not the crowd she'd expected. She was at a loss. She'd put ads in the paper, there had been signs up at the cafe for a month touting the grand opening. Her regulars had even seemed excited.

Katherine came up to her. "I don't understand. I thought we'd have a great crowd."

"I don't know, Kat. I just don't know." Keely could hear the defeat in her voice.

Hunt came in from the patio where he'd been sitting nursing a beer. He'd said he wanted to stick around tonight in case he was needed. Needed for what? She probably could have run the cafe all by herself tonight with the few people that had come in.

"You doing okay?"

"Sure. Just peachy." Keely tried to keep the disappointment from bubbling over, because she was just on the edge of tears.

Hunt came around behind the counter and gave her a quick hug. "I'm not sure where everyone is. I'd figured you'd be packed."

Keely just nodded, wiping off the counter even though no one had sat at it all evening.

Just then Bella and Owen came into the cafe, holding hands, all smiles. They stopped and looked around the almost empty cafe. Jenny, Clay, and his mother, Greta, came in right after them.

She watched as Becky Lee went over to greet them.

She turned to Hunt and Katherine with a weak smile. "Well, at least they'll have their choice of tables."

She watched as Jenny handed Becky Lee a piece of paper. Then Bella snatched the paper and crumpled it into a ball, an angry look crossing her face. Becky Lee took the crumbled paper and headed back over to the counter.

"This is our problem." Becky Lee smoothed out the paper and handed it to Keely. "It's tonight... at Camille's mama's house."

Keely looked down at the flier.

Huge BBQ to kick off Summerfest.
Free Food and Beer.
Everyone is invited.

Katherine took the paper from Keely and read it. "What? Like Camille had anything to do with Summerfest. You know she did this deliberately on our opening night." Katherine's eyes glistened with anger.

Keely's heart sank. She knew Camille could be catty. Annoying. But it did look like she'd gone out of her way to sabotage their opening.

"Let me see that." Hunt reached over and took the flier. He let out a low whistle. "Wow, she does know how to make a statement."

"Jenny said Camille went to the school and announced the barbecue at the closing assembly. Said it was a last minute thing. She even heard Luke, the DJ on the local radio station, talking about it. You remember Luke. That guy Camille dated a few years back? Yes, that Luke." Becky rolled her eyes. "Then Jenny saw this flier on her way in."

Hunt shook his head. "When Camille's mama throws a shindig, everyone is eager to go. She pulls out all the stops. Her barbecues are epic."

"That little…" Katherine balled up the flier. "I know she can be kind of all mean girlish, but I didn't see anything like this coming."

"I'm so sorry, Keely. I can't believe she'd do this." Hunt draped his arm around Keely's shoulder.

"I don't want your sympathy." Keely shrugged Hunt's arm off. "It is what it is. Camille has always known how to make my life miserable. She's exceeded my wildest expectations this time."

Camille had totally caught her by surprise this time. She'd never underestimate the woman again. What she couldn't understand was why Camille would do this. What the heck had she ever done to Camille? Or maybe Camille just liked to toy with people, prove her superiority, prove she could win. Keely swiped at the already clean counter again as disappointment swept through her.

Keely looked up to see her mother come through the door. She braced herself, waiting for what she was sure was coming.

Her mother stalked over to the counter. "What's going on? No one is here." Her voice rang out across the cafe.

"Camille's mother decided to throw one of her legendary barbecues. I would imagine most of the town is out there at their plantation." Keely faced her mother.

"Well, I told you this patio thing was nonsense. It made absolutely no difference, didn't bring in a crowd, now did it?"

"Mother, that's not fair. We had no idea Camille would pull a stunt like this. Maybe she ruined the opening, but in the long run, the patio is still a fabulous idea for the cafe." Katherine rose to her sister's defense.

"Waste of good money. I told you so."

Keely looked at her mother. The woman who would never be happy with anything Keely did. Would never be proud of her. Would never forgive her.

"You did tell me so, Mother, you did." Keely turned and walked back into her office.

Hunt wanted to strangle Camille, not that it would help anything. She'd already done her damage to Keely's grand opening of the patio. He'd no doubt it was a deliberate move on Camille's part.

At least the rest of Summerfest went off without a hitch. Tourists filled the town. The parade was a roaring success. Main Street was crowded with people milling around, shopping and enjoying perfect weather. He'd been glad to see a steady flow of people through Magnolia Cafe all during the festival. At least that part had worked out.

Hunt walked through the city park during the ice

cream social, enjoying a large butter pecan ice cream cone. He ran into Bella and Katherine near the gazebo.

"Congrats, ladies. It looks like all your hard work paid off. Summerfest appears to be a megahit."

"Thanks, Hunt. I'm glad to see so many people came to town for it." Katherine looked around at the crowded park. "And did you see how busy the cafe is, too? At least Keely is happy about that."

"I did pop in there and check on her. She was crazy busy, even the patio was full of people either waiting for tables, or having a break and a drink."

"There is already talk about making Summerfest an annual event." Bella threw out her arm. "Just look at all these people. I'm so pleased."

"You two should be proud of yourselves."

"Well, I've got to head back to my shop. It's insanely busy there. I'm trying to pop in there and still come out here and check on festival things. It's been a crazy weekend." Bella turned to Katherine. "You headed back to the cafe?"

"I am."

The two women headed down the pathway out of the park and back onto Main Street. Hunt wandered around a bit, saying hi to people he knew, feeling a bit lost, like he didn't quite belong.

"Well, hi there, Hunt."

He'd recognize that voice anywhere. He slowly turned around. "Camille."

"Look at all the people. Who knew this many people would want to come to Comfort Crossing." Camille shrugged her shoulders. "I missed you at Mama's barbecue."

"That you did. I was at the grand opening of the Magnolia Cafe's patio."

"Oh, was that the same night?"

"Nice try, Camille. I'm sure you knew exactly what you were doing."

"I don't know what you're talking about."

"Sure you do. You've had it out for Keely since… well, since as long as I can remember."

"Oh, you exaggerate. I hardly keep up with what's going on in her life."

"And yet, you did."

"Seriously, Hunt. I don't know how you can accuse me of something like that. Her life just doesn't even *interest* me."

He could see the lie, clearly spread across her face. "So what is it about Keely that gets to you, anyway?"

Camille looked away for a moment, then turned back towards him. "She gets everything. Always has."

"What in the world are you talking about? Her father died, she had to take over running the family business, and her sister was in a terrible accident. How is that getting everything?"

"She got you. For her best friend in high school. You didn't have the time of day for me."

Hunt stood there with his mouth open, looking like a fool.

"You and Keely and Kevin. Always hanging out. Going places together."

"All this is about that? You've carried a grudge all these years?"

"I asked you out. More than once. You never would go with me."

"Camille, I don't remember you asking me to do anything. I don't. I'm sorry if I hurt your feelings way back then. But, be serious. I wasn't your type. I'm still not. You're the Delbert Hamilton of Hamilton hotels type. Fancy dresser. Likes to go out for expensive dinners. Drink pricey wine."

"You could be my type."

"I'm not going to change, Camille. Not for you. Not for anyone." Hunt looked at Camille in astonishment. "Look, I'm sorry. I am. But that barbecue was just mean spirited of you. It affected Keely and Katherine's livelihood, it wasn't just some game to them."

"I can have a barbecue whenever I want."

"That's the problem, Camille, you don't think about others. You just do what you want."

Camille bristled then. "Well, Hunt Robichaux, I couldn't care less about your opinion."

Just then Delbert of the Hamilton hotels walked up. "There you are, darling. I've been looking for you."

"Hi, honey. I'm getting tired of all the… *people*. What do you say we head back to Mobile?"

"That's sounds fine by me."

Camille shot Hunt one more glare and turned and walked away with Delbert. Hunt looked down at the now melted ice cream cone and tossed it in the trash.

CHAPTER 21

Bella sat with Jenny and Becky Lee at the Magnolia Cafe. They'd just finished up three slices of pie and coffee. She stabbed at the weather app on her phone, hoping it would cough up a different weather forecast. No such luck. "Jenny, I think we're going to have to plan on moving the wedding inside. I really wanted it outside at my home. It was going to be perfect, so pretty. The hurricane has wreaked quite a bit of havoc, even though it was downgraded to just a tropical storm. There's still a seventy percent chance of rain the day after tomorrow. The storms we're getting now are going to continue. I think I need to at least look at my backup plan. We can decide for sure tomorrow." Disappointment surged through Bella. She'd pictured this perfect wedding for Jenny. Outside. The arbor all decorated. A handful of family and friends. Flowers. Green bows tied on the chairs to match the color of the wedding.

"That's okay, Bella. It would have been lovely at your

217

house, and you've done so much to help me with all of this. I'm okay with moving it indoors."

"Izzy, you know that the only thing that really matters to our Jenny is that she's finally getting to marry Clay. She'd marry him anywhere, right?" Becky Lee looked at Jenny.

"I would." Jenny smiled.

"Well, we can use that cute brick storefront on Main Street. Next to Doc Baker's. It's for lease, and I talked to the owner. It's empty, and he was thrilled to let us rent it for the day for just a small fee to cover utilities. He still has them turned on while he's showing the place, so he was glad for any income. It's just down the street from Sylvia's Place for the reception."

"That sounds perfect. I never doubted you'd have a backup plan in place." Jenny nodded.

Natalie came over to their table. "Can I get you anything else?"

"No, we're fine." Bella sighed. "We're just talking about moving Jenny's wedding inside. Going to move it to that storefront near Doc Baker's, the one for rent. You know the one?"

"That used to be Milly's Alteration Shop. It does have those nice big windows in front, and the brick walls. I bet it could be made up to look really nice without much trouble."

"So, you want to run over there with me and brainstorm?" Bella looked at Natalie. "You were great with ideas for Keely's cafe. I could use someone to bounce ideas off of. We don't have much time."

"I could do that. I'm just finishing up my shift. Let me grab my raincoat and we'll run over there."

"Jenny, you want to come?"

"Becky Lee and I are meeting Mother at Sylvia's Place for a last run through of the details of the reception."

"Okay, you do that, and we'll go see what we can do with Milly's place. Don't worry about a thing. I promise I'll make it fabulous." Bella intended to keep that promise. Jenny and Clay had waited years to get married and she would give them no less than a magical, wonderful wedding. No matter what.

Natalie was surprised to see the rain had let up a bit. She stood under the overhang of Millie's shop while Bella opened the door with the key the owner had given her. She followed Bella inside.

Bella flipped on the lights, and Natalie looked around the bare room. It was a good size, certainly big enough for the small wedding that Jenny had planned. It needed a good cleaning though.

"So, what do you think?" Bella walked across the empty room, her steps echoing on the old wooden plank floor.

"It can work. I think it will be all about the lighting and flowers."

"I have an arbor my brother Gil made us. I bet we could still use it in here. Run white holiday lights through it. Twine some greenery through the arbor."

"If we go with simple and rustic, I think we can make this work." Natalie walked over to the brick wall. "Put the arbor here. Maybe flowers on each side of it? Then the aisle would stretch out that way. If I remember right, there's a room over to the side? Milly kept her finished orders in there. Then Jenny could enter from that room?"

"That should work perfectly."

"I have white wooden chairs rented, I'll change the delivery from my house to here." Bella started jotting down notes. "Oh, and get the flowers delivered here."

Natalie walked back towards the front windows. "Sure is getting dark outside. The wind is picking up, too."

"The forecast says we're in for days of storms."

Natalie turned back, surveying the space. "Let's go check that side room and make sure it will work."

Bella and Natalie crossed to the side room and opened the door. Natalie ran her hand up the wall inside the room and found the light switch. She flipped on the lights. Or should she say light? A bare bulb hung from the ceiling.

"Well, that's not going to work very well. It's so dark in here." Bella peered around the room.

"We could bring in lamps." Natalie looked around the bare room.

"Lamps. Good idea. Jenny was going to get ready at home, but if it's pouring down rain, I'm not sure that would work."

"Well, we could create a cute little dressing area in the corner."

"Oh, I have the perfect dressing table at the shop. It has a mirror. We could dress up that corner. That would work."

They crossed the room to the corner. Just then a crash echoed through the shop. Natalie started and grabbed Bella's arm.

"Sounds like the front door blew open. I'll go check." Bella turned away and started across the room.

Just then the door to the storeroom blew shut.

"Wow, it must be getting really windy out." Bella headed over to open the door.

Just then, the lights went out, plunging them into darkness.

"Bella?" Natalie peered into the darkness.

"Over here. Do you have your cell phone for a light?"

"I left it in my purse out in the main room."

"Mine is in my purse out there, too. Let me see if I can find the door."

"Be careful." Natalie heard Bella moving around in the darkness.

"Found it."

Natalie heard Bella jiggling the door.

"It won't open. It's jammed." Bella's voice drifted through the darkness.

"I'm coming over. Keep talking."

"Okay, this is me talking. I hope you can get this darn door open because I'm not liking—"

"I'm right here." Natalie reached out and Bella grabbed her arm.

"Hey, do you hear that?"

"It sounds like the alert going off on my phone." Natalie strained to hear over the wind rattling the building.

"Oh, no. That's the tornado siren going off, too. Do you hear that?" Bella clutched at Natalie's arm.

"The boys. I don't know where my boys are." Natalie heard the panic in her voice. "Hunt is supposed to pick them up."

"I'm sure he'll keep them safe."

Natalie tried to replay Bella's words over and over in her mind, reassuring herself.

"My boys are at home with the high school girl who watches them. I hope she has them somewhere safe. She's a smart girl. I'm sure she'll take care of them."

Natalie felt panic creep over her. "Let's try the door again. We need to get out of here."

She groped around until she found the door knob and tried to turn it, but even as she turned it, it did nothing. She banged on the door, which was silly, because no one else was in the building and the noise of the storm and siren was deafening.

Panic coursed through her. The boys. She hoped the boys were safe. *Hunt, don't fail me now. I know you won't. I'm depending on you.*

The tornado siren blared through the truck as Hunt drove the boys home from the market where they'd stopped after he picked them up from school. He glanced up at the sky, now displaying an ominous bruise-green cast.

"Uncle Hunt? Is that the tornado siren?" Jamie's eyes grew wide.

Hunt stopped at the next intersection and took a good look around, then glanced over at the boys. If only they hadn't stopped at the market, they'd be home safe and sound. At least they could have headed to the cellar. One more look at the sky and the roar of the winds, and he knew they weren't going to make it home in time.

Once more he had led someone—this time three someones whom he loved dearly—into danger. They were his responsibility and he was not going to fail them. Not this time.

Without thinking, he quickly turned the truck around and roared down Main Street. He pulled into a parking spot in front of the cafe, praying he could get the boys inside to safety. "Come on. Out this way. Hurry."

He scooped up Jamie and grabbed Jesse's hand. Jackson grabbed onto his shirt sleeve as they ran into the cafe. "Keely?" He called out as loud as he could, trying to be heard over the noise of the siren and wind. He turned and tugged the door shut behind him.

"Let's head towards the back, away from these windows." He rushed the boys back towards the kitchen. No one was in sight. Strange.

He scanned the area, trying to find the safest place. "Keely?" He called out again as loudly as he could.

A door swung open on the side wall. "Hunt?" Keely

poked her head out. "We're here in the pantry. Hurry. Get in."

He hustled the boys into the room and closed the door behind them. Katherine sat in her wheelchair in the back corner. "Safest place we could find. No windows."

"Natalie's not here?"

Keely shook her head no. "She left a while ago. Her shift was over."

Hunt bit his bottom lip, but concentrated on the boys. "Come on boys, let's go sit back here by Katherine, what do you say?"

The lights flickered off, then back on. They flickered once more, then darkness settled around them.

"Everyone okay?" Hunt pulled out his cell phone and shone the light around in the darkness. Jamie launched himself into his uncle's arms. "Is it going to blow us away?"

"No, we're safe here." *They'd better all be safe or Natalie was going to kill him.* The boys were his responsibility. He had to keep them safe.

"Do you think Mama's okay?" Jesse moved close and hung on Hunt's arm.

"I'm sure she is. She heard the siren just like us. She would have gone to safety."

A crashing sound came from out in the cafe.

"What's that?" Jamie held on tightly.

"Maybe a window blew out. Don't worry. We'll be fine in here." The words echoed in Hunt's brain. *Fine. They were all going to be fine.*

Keely stood leaning against the wall beside Katherine. His phone's light shut off.

"Uncle Hunt." Jamie's scared voice came through the darkness.

Hunt fumbled with his phone to switch on the light again.

"Jamie, why don't you come sit with me?" Katherine held out her hand to the boy. Jamie rushed over, climbed into her lap, and Katherine wrapped her arms around him. "We'll be okay. We're just going to stay in here until things calm down a bit."

Keely walked over to him. "You think that was the big picture window? We're going to have a mess."

"Kind of sounded like it."

Keely sighed.

Suddenly a roar like a freight train surrounded them.

"Back here in the corner." Hunt grabbed Keely and rushed her over by the boys. He huddled the boys together with Katherine and Keely, and stood in front of them, wishing he had more to block them with.

The door to the pantry flew open and some menus came flying in.

Hunt's heart pounded, it sounded like the wrath of the devil had descended upon them. The light went out on his phone again and he heard Jamie start crying.

"I'll get the light again in a minute. Just hold on. It's going to pass."

One of the boys was clinging to his arm, but he didn't dare move to mess with his phone again.

"I've got mine." Keely held out her phone with the low light illuminating the corner.

The fear in the three boys' eyes tore through him. "It will be okay." He kept his voice loud enough to be heard over the roar, his tone full of what he hoped was positive reassurance.

Just like that, the roar began to fade into the distance. He stepped back a pace, listening.

"Hey boys, this is kind of like an adventure, isn't it?" Katherine asked. "We're going have such great stories to tell about this. All about the one afternoon you all got to hide in the pantry at the cafe. At least we won't run out of food," she teased the boys, trying to break the tension.

Hunt flipped on his cell phone light and held it high.

"Uncle Hunt, are you sure our mom is okay?" Jackson looked up at him, his eyes wide.

"She's a smart woman. I'm sure she found safety."

Or foolishly headed out to make sure the boys were safe... because she wouldn't totally have trusted him to keep them safe.

CHAPTER 22

The siren ended as the roar of the wind died down.
"I'm going to go check on things. You all wait here. Boys, stay with Keely and Katherine."

"Don't leave us." Jamie's small voice quavered.

"I'll be right back. Just going to make sure it's okay for all of you to come out."

He walked out of the pantry, into the kitchen. A bit of light shone in through the one window at the far end of the kitchen. Papers and menus were scattered about. Pots were on the floor. A bag of flour had burst, showering white powder all over like a fine dusting of snow. He crossed the kitchen and headed out into the main part of the cafe. Glass was everywhere. Tables were flipped over in a pile along the back wall. Chairs were turned over this way and that, all over the cafe. The main picture window had blown out, but amazingly, the other windows were still intact. The front door was swinging wide open.

He crossed over and stepped out the door. The sight before him was staggering. Tree limbs scattered about. Windows blown out on cars and shops. A few street lamps were blown over. The building right across the street had lost its roof. Up and down the street he could see a few people coming out and beginning to check on things.

"Oh, no." Keely came up behind him. "Look at everything…"

"I thought I said to stay inside until I checked everything out."

"I don't listen very well."

"Evidently not." He wrapped an arm around her and hugged her close.

"At least we're all safe." Keely hugged him back. "Honestly, I was so glad to see your face come through that door."

Hunt smiled down at her. "I was glad to find the pantry to put the boys in. I knew I'd never make it back to Natalie's house in time."

He let go of Keely, stepped out into the middle of the street, and looked up at the roof of the cafe. "It looks like your roof is okay. At least no big holes. We'll have to get up on it to check for sure."

"If all we had was a blown out window and a mess, I'm thankful." Keely stood in the doorway.

"I need to try to reach Natalie." Hunt pulled out his cell and called his sister. He let it ring until the answering message came on. "Nat. Call me. The boys are safe. Where are you?"

He clicked off the phone.

"I would stay here and help clean up, but I've got to go find Natalie. Make sure she's okay."

"Why don't you leave the boys here with us?"

"You sure?"

"I think it would be better than dragging them around in the mess out there."

"Let me go back and tell them I'm leaving." Hunt and Keely headed back to the pantry.

"Boys, it's all over now. You can come out, but I need you to stay with Katherine and Keely for a little while. I'm going to go find your mother."

He pushed Katherine's chair out into the main part of the cafe, crunching glass as the chair rolled along. The boys followed him.

"Wow." Jesse looked around the cafe.

"You boys be careful of the glass, okay?"

"I want to come with you." Jackson stepped up and grabbed his arm.

"Jackson, I need you to help watch over your brothers. Could you do that for me?"

"Okay. I'll stay and watch 'em." Jackson nodded.

Hunt looked down at the boy and all he could see was Kevin's eyes looking back up at him.

I hear you Kevin. Loud and clear, buddy. I'll go find her and make sure she's safe.

Owen pushed through the door of the carriage house. It had taken him what seemed like hours to get here because the streets were covered in limbs. He'd finally abandoned his car and ran the rest of the way.

"Bella?"

He stood in the room looking around, willing Bella to appear in front of him.

Jeremy came out of Bella's bedroom with his hand firmly holding Timmy's.

"Owen?" Timmy raced over and threw himself into Owen's arms.

Owen stumbled back but caught the boy firmly in a hug. "You okay?"

"We're fine. But Mom's not here." Timmy looked up at him, his eyes wide. Tracks ran down his cheeks from recent tears.

The sitter came up behind Jeremy. "We're all fine. I took the boys into the closet when we heard the sirens."

"Smart thinking. I'm sure Bella was glad she could count on you."

Jeremy walked up to him. "Mr. Campbell, do you think you can find my mom?"

"I sure will, Jeremy. I sure will. You two stay here with your sitter, and I'll bring your mom back here as quickly as I can, okay?"

Owen looked at the two boys and his heart swelled. They were safe. He'd been so worried about them and Bella. All of this was so new to him. He'd always only had to take care of himself, worry about himself or at the most his employees. Nothing like the feelings that were coursing through him now at the thought of anything happening to Bella or the boys.

"Jeremy, you think you can find a piece of paper and

write down my phone number? Then you call if you hear anything at all about your mother, okay?"

"I can do that." Jeremy went over to the counter, grabbed a pen and paper, and wrote down the number.

"I'm going to go now and find her. I'll bring her back, safe and sound." Owen walked away from the carriage house and saw both boys' faces pressed against the window, watching him leave. He hoped he'd just made a promise he could keep.

He decided to try the cafe first and hurried down the street.

Owen rushed through the open door of the cafe. "I can't find Bella. Does anyone know where she is? She isn't at her house or her shop. Her boys are at her house with a babysitter and they're okay, but Bella's not there. I've tried calling and she's not picking up."

"She was here earlier, but she left." Keely walked over to him.

Tension swept through Owen and settled in his stomach. He was not used to feeling so helpless. He was the man in control. Making decisions. Making things happen. But now, he couldn't even find the woman he loved. "I can't find her anywhere."

"I'm sure she's okay. She probably ducked in somewhere to stay safe," Keely assured him.

"Right. I'm sure you're right. But where is she? I'd think she would have raced home to check on the boys.

I told the sitter to call me immediately if Bella showed up."

Becky Lee walked up behind him. "I came to see how you fared, Keely."

"Have you seen Bella?" Owen knew he should stay calm, but he couldn't help himself, he was beginning to panic. Where was she?

"She and Natalie went to look at a place they wanted to use for Jenny's wedding."

"Natalie is with Bella?" Hunt walked up and stood by Becky Lee. "Where did they go to look?"

"It's the shop for lease down the street. Next to Doc Baker's, the vet."

"Let's go." Owen rushed out the door with Hunt right on his heels. They ran down the street, avoiding blown over trash receptacles, a sparking streetlight, and a kid's bicycle tangled up in some fencing. His heart plummeted when he saw a few buildings had tumbled in on themselves. The tornado seemed to skip around and pick and choose what to destroy.

"There." Hunt pointed.

A building with a for lease sign stood, thankfully in good condition, right next to Doc Baker's clinic. Owen opened the door and called out. "Bella?"

Hunt came up behind him. "Natalie? You here?"

"Owen. In here."

He heard pounding coming from the back of the building. He and Hunt hurried toward the sound. Owen tugged on the door. Nothing.

"Is Natalie in there?" Hunt called out.

"I'm here. We're fine. The door is stuck."

"We'll get you out of there. Hang on."

Hunt looked at the door. "The hinges are on the outside, thank goodness." He took out his pocket knife and pried the pins out of the hinges, and Owen helped him pull the door off the frame.

Bella came tumbling out and rushed into Owen's arms. He held her close and stroked her hair. "Bella. You gave me such a scare." His heart was still hammering in his chest, he could seem to hold her close enough.

"The boys, I have to go find the boys."

"They're fine. I checked on them."

Bella collapsed against him then, her tears falling onto his shirt. "I was so worried and I couldn't do anything locked in that darn room."

"Sh, it's okay. It's all over now."

He looked over at Hunt, who held his sister in a bear hug.

"Hunt, the boys? Are they okay?" Natalie asked.

"They are. We hid out in the pantry at the cafe. They'll have such stories to tell you."

"I knew you would keep them safe. I just knew it."

Hunt looked at his sister in surprise. "You did?"

"Of course, you'd never let me down on something so important. Take me there, I need to see them." Natalie stepped out of her brother's arms and tugged on his hand. "Let's go."

"You two okay?" Hunt looked over at Owen and Bella.

"Yes, go." Owen nodded.

Bella leaned against Owen. "I didn't know when anyone would find us. It sounded like the whole building was going to come crashing down on us. I've never heard a sound like that… like a train headed straight for us."

"I'm sorry I wasn't here with you."

"Well, the good thing is, since you weren't here you could come rescue us. Wouldn't have done us much good if you'd been locked in there with us."

"I guess not." He smiled down at Bella, so glad to have her safe in his arms. He never wanted to let her go. Ever.

Crazy thoughts whirled around in his head. All the reasons that he shouldn't open his mouth, shouldn't do this, shouldn't ask this…

He dropped to one knee and took Bella's hand. "Bella, will you marry me?"

Bella looked down at Owen, unable to hide her surprise. Her heart banged in her chest. Had he just asked her to marry him?

"I know this isn't the most romantic way to ask you. I'll make that up to you, I promise, but I don't ever, ever want to lose you. I love you. I want to spend the rest of my life with you."

Bella stood there silent, unable to speak.

"Are you going to answer me?"

"Owen, I…" She dropped down to her knees beside him and threw herself into his arms.

"I will marry you. Yes." She buried her face in his neck, her hot tears trailing down and soaking his collar.

"Hm, Bella, you've made me the happiest man in the world." He stood up and pulled her up with him.

"And you, Mr. Campbell, you've made me the happiest woman. I do so love you, you know."

"I don't want to wait either. I want to be married right away. Does that work for you?"

"That works fine. You never know what's going to happen in life, I don't plan on wasting a day of it." Bella tipped her face up and kissed him.

Owen touched her face, her beautiful face. He brushed her hair back and kissed her again. She did that little half-sigh that drove him crazy. He pulled back and laughed. "Come on. I'm going to take you home to your boys."

He walked her home through the battered streets of Comfort Crossing. The boys came running out of the carriage house before he even got Bella to the door.

"Mom." Timmy wrapped his arms around Bella.

"Mom, you're safe. Where were you?" Jeremy hugged her.

"I was locked in a room in a building on Main Street. Owen found me and got me out."

Jeremy looked up at Owen like he was some kind of hero. "Thank you Mr. Campbell—Owen—for finding my mom."

"You're welcome, son. Kind of glad to have her back with us, myself."

Bella smiled at him and took his hand. "Come on, let's all go inside. We have lots to talk about."

CHAPTER 23

K eely looked out the door and down the street. Weirdly, a trampoline rested against a lamppost. A few buildings looked like they were totally destroyed. They were so lucky at the cafe. She wondered if their house had damage, though a police officer had come by to check on them and said most of the damage was along Main Street. She'd better call and check on her mother.

Hunt and Natalie came through the door right then. Jamie launched himself into his mother's arms. "Mom."

Jesse and Jackson came running up from the back room and Natalie wrapped all three boys in a hug.

"You should have seen Uncle Hunt. He got us all out of the truck and into the cafe. Miss Katherine and Miss Keely had us come back with them in the pantry." Jesse danced around in front of his mother.

"It was dark," Jamie added.

"But Uncle Hunt used his phone to light the room.

It sounded like a train was going to squash us like a bug." Jackson added to the story.

"I'm just glad you're safe." Natalie still held Jamie in her arms.

"Miss Katherine kept us safe, too. She let me sit on her lap. She said we're going to have big stories to tell now." Jamie squirmed out of his mother's arms and went to stand by Katherine.

"Hunt, I think it's time you talked to Katherine and Keely."

Keely watched as a look went from Natalie to Hunt. He nodded.

"I'm going to take the boys home. I think now is as good as any time to tell Katherine the truth." Natalie turned to the sisters. "Thanks for helping to keep my boys safe."

"Let's go boys. We're going to walk. It appears Uncle Hunt parked the truck under a tree that decided to crash through the windshield." Natalie herded her boys out the door.

"What was Natalie talking about?" Keely turned to Hunt.

Hunt pulled a chair over to sit next to Katherine. "I have something to tell you. It should have been told long ago. It wasn't mine to tell, but now that Natalie said it's okay, I'll tell you the truth about your accident."

"What are you talking about?" Keely came over and sat beside them.

"The accident. It was Kevin's fault."

"What do you mean?" Keely interrupted him.

"Kevin was driving home from work that night. He

fell asleep at the wheel and swerved into the other lane at an oncoming car. He said he looked in his rearview mirror and thought the other car was okay. He left the next day to go to stay with his uncle for the summer. When he came back, he heard about the accident."

"That's why he was always doing stuff for us, wasn't it?" Keely thought of the many times Kevin had helped them out. She'd thought he'd just felt sorry for them.

"The accident wasn't Kevin's fault." Katherine put her hand on Hunt's. "It was mine."

"No, he said he drifted over to the oncoming lane."

"Oh, he did. I didn't know that was him. But I swerved to miss him. That didn't cause the accident. I reached over after that to put a CD in the player in the car. I dropped the disc and leaned over to get it. I lost control of the car. Not Kevin's fault. Not at all."

"So it had nothing to do with Kevin?" He turned to Keely. "And it wasn't your fault for not letting her use your car. Had nothing to do with the stick shift."

"What? You thought my accident was your fault?" Katherine turned to her sister.

"You wanted my car that night and I wouldn't let you drive it because of our silly fight over that red sweater. I know you weren't comfortable driving Father's manual transmission."

"Oh, Keely. None of this was your fault either. I did fine with Father's car. I would never have parallel parked it on a hill or anything, but I could drive it just fine. I was just young and made a poor choice. I should have kept my eyes on the road, not messing with the CDs." Katherine shook her head. "I didn't know you blamed yourself. Mother knew the truth. I told both Mother and Father what had happened. I thought you knew and were just being kind to me not to throw it in my face what a stupid thing I did."

Keely sat back and her whole life tilted off axis. Everything she'd believed, the reasons for taking over the cafe… it was all… wrong. Her mother had known the truth too, about the cause of the accident, about the fact her father had refused to take responsibility for his heart problems.

Why had she spent all these years trying to make her mother happy? Gain her approval. Win her mother's forgiveness. Forgiveness that wasn't needed in the first place.

"Are you okay?" Hunt locked his gaze on her.

"You know what? I think I am. For the first time in a long time, I think I am."

Hunt helped Keely board up the window to the cafe and clean up the broken glass. They'd picked up scattered menus, napkins, and broken dishes. He'd mopped the floor, twice, and uprighted tables and chairs. Keely had finally sent Katherine and Becky Lee home.

"I'm just going to run home for a few minutes. It's getting dark, and I want to check on Natalie and the boys. I'll be back as quick as I can."

"You don't have to come back. It's okay." Keely stood in the middle of the cafe with a smudge of dirt across her cheek and a tired look etched across her face.

"No, I'm coming back. Do you want to take a break and walk over there with me? A break would do you good."

"I don't know. There is so much still to do."

"We'll be back. Come with me." He held out his hand to her.

Keely nodded and placed her hand in his. They walked out onto the street. Keely stopped and slowly looked around. He followed her gaze. Across the street, Doc Baker was helping the lady who owned the dress shop. He was nailing a piece of plywood on the front window of her shop. Bella's brother, Gil, had gone through town with sheets of plywood from his hardware store, giving them to anyone who needed to board up windows. A group of high school kids were collecting limbs and debris from the streets and sidewalks. A handful of men were up on top of the roof of the store on the corner, securing blue tarps to cover a gaping hole.

She turned to Hunt. "You see that? That is Comfort Crossing at its best. Helping each other. Pulling together. I know I've always said I want to travel, and I do, but this town? I love this town. I'm just now realizing how much. I can't imagine ever living somewhere else. I would still always want to call Comfort Crossing home."

He looked at the townsfolk helping others, already cleaning up the mess the storm had wreaked on the town. She was right, it was a good place to call home. A place where neighbors helped neighbors, and even a tornado couldn't keep them down for long.

They held hands, and he led her down the streets to

Natalie's house. The street lights that normally would have come on by now, stood as silent sentries, lining the streets. As they got to Natalie's house he was glad to see there wasn't much more damage than a few limbs he'd have to cut up.

He opened the front door and held it open for Keely to enter. "Natalie?"

"I'm back here."

Hunt and Keely crossed to the kitchen. Natalie sat at the table in the flickering candle light, sipping tea.

"Hi, you two. Want some hot tea? I remembered Kevin had a camp stove. I used it to cook for the boys and made some tea. Are you hungry? Nothing fancy, but I have left over mac and cheese."

"That would be really nice." Keely sank into a chair at the kitchen table, and Hunt sat beside her.

Natalie walked over and grabbed two bowls of macaroni and cheese and some hot tea.

"Thanks, sis." He took a bite of the meal. "Where are the boys?"

"They're upstairs making a tent out of blankets and sheets. They have a couple of flashlights and they're pretending they're camping."

Hunt shook his head. "They sure bounce back from things quickly, don't they?"

"Faster than I do. I'm exhausted."

"Nat, now that we're here, I need to tell you something." He looked over at Keely, then Natalie. "It's about Kevin. He didn't cause Katherine's accident."

"What?"

"Katherine said she remembers a car swerving into

her lane the night of the accident, but she avoided it. A little bit down the road she was trying to put a CD into the player, and she dropped the disc. She leaned over to get it and lost control of the car. It had nothing to do with Kevin."

The light danced across Natalie's cheeks and tears started to roll. "Oh. If only Kevin could have known that. All those years of blaming himself. All the guilt and responsibility he took on his shoulders."

Just then the kitchen door blew open and a gust of wind snuffed out the candles.

I hear you buddy. You know now, don't you?

Hunt reached for the matchbook on the table and lit the candles again.

"I wish he could have known it wasn't his fault. I'm sure it ate away at him all the time. I sure know how he felt." Keely's voice was low.

"He changed so much after the accident. It must have haunted him every day." Natalie wiped at her tears. "Gosh, I miss him so much."

"I know you do, sis. I'm sorry."

Natalie let out a long sigh. "It's been so nice having you here for a while. Another adult person to talk to. You've been such a great help, but I know you've been getting job offers for photo assignments. It's time you got on with your life. The boys and I will be fine. We will."

Keely looked over at him, searching his face for his reaction to Natalie's words, obviously waiting to hear what he'd say, because he knew he'd kept repeating to anyone who asked that he was leaving after Summerfest.

"I don't know, Nat. It's going to be hard to leave. I'm kind of getting used to being here. I think the boys are getting used to me being around. I even remembered to go to the market today." Hunt shook his head. "Of course the groceries are still in the truck with windshield glass all over them. I did cover the windshield up earlier today though. We'll get it fixed as soon as possible. I'll see what I can salvage of the food and bring it back with me tonight."

Just then the boys came racing down the stairs.

"Uncle Hunt. Uncle Hunt." Jamie launched himself into this uncle's arms. "You saved us today, didn't you?"

"Well, I…"

"Yes, boys. Your uncle took very good care of you today. Kept you safe. I knew he would." Natalie wrapped an arm around Jesse, who came and stood by her side.

"He was awesome, wasn't he Miss Keely? Mom, should have seen him turn the truck around and get us into the Magnolia Cafe. He hid us in the pantry with Miss Keely and Miss Katherine." Jackson stood by the table.

"That was quick thinking on his part."

"He stood over all of us when the door blew open to the pantry so we wouldn't get hit with the stuff blowing around." Jesse chimed in to the storytelling.

Natalie reached over and covered his hand. "I can never thank you enough for keeping the boys safe. I knew I could depend on you."

Hunt looked at the boys and Natalie in the dancing light from the candles. He'd spent so many years just dropping into town for a few days at a time in between assignments. He'd forgotten what it was like to feel like this. Like he was part of a family. Like he belonged.

And he realized he liked the feeling.

He liked it quite a bit, actually. He liked helping Natalie and the boys and was no longer willing to run from any and all responsibility. It had felt right to be there for the boys, for Natalie. He looked at Keely sitting silently at the table.

And it felt right to be there for Keely.

He leaned back in his chair. "You know what? I don't think I'm going to head out after all."

"You're going to stay in Comfort Crossing?" Jamie jumped up and down. "Yes."

"I am going to stay. Might move out and find a place of my own, but I'm going to stay in town." He turned to Keely and took her hand in his, looking directly into her eyes. "How do you feel about that? Would you like me to stay?"

Keely sat silently, then a smile slowly spread across her face. "I would. I'd like that very much."

He leaned over and kissed her quickly on the lips.

"Seriously, Uncle Hunt. Right here in front of the little kids?" Jackson rolled his eyes.

"I'm not a little kid," Jamie retorted.

Natalie stood up, grinned at Hunt, and turned to the boys. "How about you show me the fort you made?"

The boys led her up the stairs with shouts of "Me first!" and Jamie still exclaiming he wasn't a little kid.

"Hunt, are you sure about this?"

"I am so sure. I want to stay here. I want to be here

for Natalie and the boys." He paused for a moment gathering his courage. "And I want to be here for you. I'm crazy about you."

He reached over and brushed a wisp of hair away from her face and traced his finger along her check. "Keely, I've fallen in love with you."

"I love you, too, Hunt Robichaux."

His heart soared. He stood up and took her in his arms, twirling her around. Keely laughed out loud.

"You're crazy."

"Crazy about you."

He set her back down on the floor. "So, I have no idea what I'm going to do, but I'll figure something out. I could do more construction, I enjoy that. I've wanted to do up a photography book from my travels."

"I could always go with you on a few assignments. I think Katherine could take over the cafe when we're gone. It's time I accept her help. Mother won't be happy, but then for the first time in my adult life, I'm not setting out to please my mother. As you kept telling me —and I'm willing to listen to now—we all make choices."

"And I choose you." Hunt took both her hands in his, his heart happy and his future looking bright. "And even if we travel some, Comfort Crossing will always be our home."

CHAPTER 24

"After the tornado cancelled our wedding last month, Clay almost had me convinced we should run off and elope." Jenny stood in front of the full length mirror at Bella's house. "He wasn't much on waiting four more weeks."

"I, for one, am very glad he waited." Becky Lee came up behind Jenny and gave her a quick hug. "You look beautiful. The wedding is going to be fabulous."

Jenny stepped away from the mirror and Becky Lee stood in front of it, critically looking at herself. "I sure didn't think I'd be the only bridesmaid, though."

"I didn't think you would be either." Bella looked down at her own wedding dress and ran her hand over the delicate lace. "But a double wedding seemed like the most logical solution, didn't it?"

Jenny laughed. "Well, since you'd already planned the wedding, it seemed only fair to share it with you once you and Owen decided to get married."

247

Bella grinned. "I had all that planning already finished for your interrupted wedding. Just added a few more guests, more food at the reception, and presto, we have a double wedding."

Jenny's eyes sparkled. "I'm so happy for you and Owen."

"And I'm so glad we're finally going to see you and Clay married." Bella's heart was filled with love and gratitude for her friends and full of love for Owen. Even with all the rush of the preparations, a peace spread through her.

"The wedding is going to be magical. The arbor is lovely. The chairs have those darling mint green bows tied on them. The hydrangeas everywhere. Bella, you've outdone yourself." Becky Lee turned and walked over to her friends. "I tell y'all, it's about time we're seeing these weddings."

Bella peeked out the window and saw Owen and Clay standing by the arbor with Pastor Adam. Owen shifted back and forth, twisting his watch. She smiled. Owen's brother, Jake, leaned over and said something to him, and Owen nodded. It wasn't often she saw the cool businessman acting nervous. She was nervous herself… only she wasn't. Excited might be a better word. She smoothed the skirt of her wedding dress again.

The music started playing outside in Bella's garden. Her heart did a quick flip of joy. She was marrying Owen. Jenny and Clay were finally going to be together.

"Okay, here we go." Becky Lee stood in the doorway and turned to smile back at her friends, then headed out the door and started down the aisle.

Bella took Jenny's hand in hers.

Jenny squeezed her hand and smiled. "You ready?"

Bella nodded.

Jenny and Bella walked down the aisle to their very own happily-ever-afters.

Thank you for reading my story. I hope you enjoyed it. Sign up for my newsletter to be updated with information on new releases, promotions, and give-aways. The signup is at my website, kaycorrell.com.

Reviews help other readers find new books. I always appreciate when my readers take time to leave an honest review.

I love to hear from my readers. Feel free to contact me at authorcontact@kaycorrell.com

COMFORT CROSSING ~ THE SERIES

The Shop on Main - Book One

The Memory Box - Book Two

The Christmas Cottage - A Holiday Novella (Book 2.5)

The Letter - Book Three

The Christmas Scarf - A Holiday Novella (Book 3.5)

The Magnolia Cafe - Book Four

The Unexpected Wedding - Book Five

The Wedding in the Grove (crossover short story between series - Josephine and Paul from The Letter.)

LIGHTHOUSE POINT ~ THE SERIES

ABOUT THE AUTHOR

Kay Correll writes stories that are a cross between contemporary romance and women's fiction. She likes her books with a healthy dose of happily ever after. Her stories are set in the fictional small towns of Comfort Crossing, Mississippi and Belle Island, Florida. While her books are a series, each one can be read as a stand-alone story.

Kay lives in the Midwest of the U.S. and can often be found out and about with her camera, taking a myriad of photographs which she likes to incorporate into her book covers. When not lost in her writing or photography, she can be found spending time with her ever-supportive husband, knitting, or playing with her puppies—two cavaliers and one naughty but adorable Australian shepherd. Kay and her husband also love to travel. When it comes to vacation time, she is torn between a nice trip to the beach or the mountains—but the mountains only get considered in the summer—she swears she's allergic to snow.

Learn more about Kay and her books at kaycorrell.com

While you're there, sign up for her newsletter to hear about new releases, sales, and giveaways.

WHERE TO FIND ME:
kaycorrell.com
authorcontact@kaycorrell.com

Made in the USA
Coppell, TX
07 August 2021